ONE MAN'S HONOUR

TERRY M. DUNN

Terry M. Dunn
2022

Published by Daneburyverse Books
Printed by Book Printing UK
Remus House, Coltsfoot Drive, Peterborough PE2 9BF
ISBN 978-1-9162657-1-4

To all those who urged me to make the tall man live again.

Thanks.

3,510 BC

1

The Chieftain stood outside the threshold of his house and looked down at the village, laid out on the gently sloping ground below him. From his vantage point on the higher ground of the north-west quarter of the hillfort he could see practically all of the family huts, including the larger shrine hut of the Earth Goddess in the centre of the village of Danebury. Or Dane-bre, as the occupants here called it.

Surrounding the village and the entire top of the hill was a palisade wall and an external ditch, deep, wide and steep sided. Beyond that, on the slopes that led to the valley floor and eventually to the edge of the great forest, the green pastures beyond the village's patchwork of crop fields were dotted with the scattered flock of sheep that was so important to the well being of the people of Danebury. The Chieftain's people.

But for the moment he didn't see any of the pleasant, sweeping vista before him. From his lofty observation point where he had built his house and now lived, a place from where he had always watched the village, he saw in his mind's eye the eventful day when a stranger had come to Danebury.

A striking looking man to the inhabitants of the village and so different from the rest of the people of the Earth Goddess, that when he first appeared he made them uneasy, wary and perhaps even a little frightened. A strange man with strange ways. So much taller, bulkier and stronger than all the other men of this land that it did not even seem possible that he could be born of a woman. He was also dressed in strange, camouflage patterned clothing and carried with him many curious and mysterious objects. He had filled the local people of the village with distrust and fear, a fear of the unknown. They had never seen his like before.

And they never would again, for this was the time of the ascent of man. The early years that people would look back at and call the time of the young, for no one ever lived long enough to grow old. 25 years was considered mature, 30 old. 35 was positively ancient and very rarely reached. There was as yet no metal on the land, apart from the few small pieces that the stranger had brought with him on his astounding journey from his former life, to the life he now lived.

At this the Chieftain smiled because only the tall man, this stranger in a strange land, knew the actual time in which they now lived.

To everyone else but him this was a land before time.

The stranger's name was Shaun Parrish, formerly of the 2nd Battalion the Light Infantry, based in the cathedral city of Winchester. Eight years a soldier, Private Parrish was the unfortunate victim of an accident on Salisbury Plain in the summer of 1988. An accident involving a secret, experimental machine that could cross the normally uncrossable barrier of time itself. Held in the machines grip, Parrish was hurled back down the years to arrive totally unprepared into this land of the young. But there was no going back, it was a one way trip and Parrish found himself trapped in the land before time, 3,500 years before the birth of Christ!

At first it had been hard on Parrish. Very hard. But he had learned to adjust. He had needed to, mistakes here could prove costly. Death was sometimes only a heartbeat away in this hostile Neolithic landscape. It had taken the tall stranger a long time just to become accepted by the people of Danebury.

He had needed to learn their language, their customs and to understand their religion. What had started with crushing despair and a feeling of utter, smothering and suffocating loneliness upon realizing that he had lost forever his modern life in the 20th Century, had then become an astounding, fascinating and rewarding journey of discovery as Parrish gradually melded into and became an intrinsic part of Danebury. Receptive to and a participant in the varied events in the Neolithic life of a village in prehistoric Southern England.

The Chieftain smiled at the recollection of some of the events that had drawn the tall stranger slowly yet inexorably into the very fabric of the village and its people until he was one of them, until he affected them as much as they affected him. Parrish had befriended people, helped them as individuals and helped the village as a whole and had at last come to fully accept life in Neolithic Britain. Their way had become his and he had at times been instrumental in key events over the last two years, his time in this land of the young. Parrish had been involved in battles, taken a wife and witnessed mysterious and magical religious rituals, even becoming sympathetic towards the people's worship of their Earth goddess, Dannu.

Eventually, being respected by the warriors of Danebury, admired by the children and loved by the downtrodden women of the village, the people had, in the aftermath of a potentially disastrous battle that had raged just beyond the walls of the hillfort, finally paid Parrish the ultimate accolade.

All this the Chieftain saw in his mind's eye as he looked out, reflecting on the past events. Now the sun shone down from a clear sky, warming the Stone Age landscape, a landscape still free of man's mass destruction, deformation, abuse and exploitation, shone down through a smog and pollution free sky. The air was sweet and the land green and fertile.

Here, in this small part of the Neolithic landscape where the Chieftain of Danebury's power was absolute, the people under his charge were happy and contented. Looking out over his village and his people, the Chieftain smiled. Life was good.

A proud, confident figure suddenly appeared from between the huts and began striding purposefully up the slope towards where the Chieftain stood, aware of his leader's eyes on him. He knew the Chieftain missed nothing. It was well known that the man's stare could at times be almost piercing.

The Chieftains gaze swept over the familiar features of the approaching man, taking in the short, almost stocky stature that was common among the male adults of Neolithic Britain. Perhaps five feet three inches in height but definitely not much more, the warrior wore the traditional leather buckskins of the times and across his back draped the calf length woollen cape that was common to and almost exclusively worn only by the people of Danebury. Whenever the cape swept back as the warrior walked, it briefly revealed a keen edged flint dagger tucked into the belt of his tunic. The man's face was unforgettable. Above his hawk like eyes, in a heavy black line reaching almost from temple to temple, was a single great slash of bushy eyebrows.

But even this feature was secondary to the man's nose. It was badly broken and misshapen, the result of a disagreement with the tall stranger during his early days in the village. As this striking individual drew nearer he offered the Chieftain a broad, toothy grin.

The man's name was Klud. The many tattoos he wore with pride marked him as a great warrior among his people. He was the holder of many heads, human skulls proudly displayed as trophies on the walls of his stall in the shrine house of the Earth Goddess in the centre of the village, proving him the victor of many battles. Even so, he considered himself vastly inferior to his Chieftain, who he knew beyond doubt was brave, clever, wise and also the holder of many skulls of his own. Yet he was honoured to call this great man his friend. They had shared many experiences together and he was sure they would share many more, for the Chieftain was an extraordinary man. Around him extraordinary things happened.

The Chieftain watched Klud approach. The appreciation he knew Klud had for him was returned in equal measure. When he had first met the Danebury warrior he'd thought him no more than a Neolithic nitwit. Loutish and a brute, he appeared to be simply an insensitive thug. He was wrong. Through their shared experiences the two men had become great friends and comrades in arms. Klud had even been offered the position of Chieftain, the highest possible honour, but had refused it in preference to serving as the strong right hand of the new Chieftain. He was always on hand, sometimes to offer the great man simple words of advice or occasionally to gently steer him to the right decision whenever a problem arose concerning the smooth running of the village that the Chieftain was not sure how to solve correctly. For as great as the Chieftain was, he was sometimes woefully inadequate in his knowledge of many of the day to day running of Neolithic village life.

The whole village knew this and yet they had still elected him to the high position he now held. He was proud to be chosen by the people, their proof of the faith they had in him, and was always grateful for Klud's assistance in his times of indecision. It was always his wish to do the right thing for the continued welfare of his village. The people knew this and were, in turn, proud of their caring and protecting leader.

The Chieftain returned the Neolithic man's grin as Klud finally stepped up and stood beside him. It was the place where he believed Dannu had always meant him to be. Turning to stare down into the village also, he surveyed the collection of circular, thatched huts spread out below them in the sunshine, trying to think the Chieftains thoughts. He could not. The great man knew things that no one else knew.

"What are you thinking, Parrish?" Klud asked finally.

The Chieftain turned and looked down at his shorter friend. "I was remembering when I first came to this place."

"Yes." At that Klud inadvertently fingered his misshapen nose. The men's eyes met and they both laughed. The Neolithic man nodded.

"There were some dark times my friend but now the sun shines. The crops grow, children play, you are Chieftain and Dannu smiles on us. Life is good."

"I was just thinking the same thing."

The swishing back of the door blanket that covered the entrance behind them made both men turn. Juli stood in the doorway and bowed deeply to the two men.

Klud didn't appear even to notice the woman's acknowledgment. Why should he? He was a warrior and she was nothing but a female. Parrish however smiled broadly down at his diminutive wife. Klud certainly noticed this though and shook his head sadly. Neither he nor any of the other men of Danebury could understand the strange attitude that the Chieftain had towards his plus the fact that for some reason he would only take one wife. He must surely know that women were only here to serve and to bear sons. They were gifts by Dannu to the men who lived upon her land, yet sometimes Parrish seemed almost respectful to his wife. Even so, Klud never spoke of it. So long as it did not affect the running of the village and kept Parrish happy, he felt it not necessary to correct him.

Juli understood this equally as well as Klud and did not return her husband's smile. In the privacy of their house it would have been different. There her husband had encouraged her to become more relaxed and open, to be free to speak and even to ask questions, normally things that if any lowly woman dared to do in these Neolithic times would be considered great insults and severely punishable.

Women were indeed grossly subservient to the men of the

village. They were the work horses, taking care of all the day to day chores and menial tasks, the making of clothing, cooking and raising the children. It was one of the things that Parrish found most objectionable about the primitive times in which he now lived. He had put a lot of time and effort into bringing Juli at least a part way out from under the male oppression that threatened to crush the women here. Juli was grateful for this and enjoyed her new found if somewhat limited sense of freedom. It also made life more difficult for her because she had to be constantly on her guard so as not to let slip an indiscretion beyond the confines of their house and get herself into trouble, trouble that could also affect her husband, the Chieftain.

Parrish was blissfully unaware of her personal struggle but he was aware of the normally unseen subculture that the women of the land had developed. A clandestine network of mutual help between them all. They simply tried their best to look out for one another, helping other women who got into difficulties, assisting mostly by passing goods back and forth among each other to aid in the smooth running of individual family units. The men of the village seemed totally oblivious to these goings on. All that was apart from Parrish. He knew but never said anything. The women knew he knew and were grateful for his discretion.

Parrish smiled down at Juli and thought her beautiful. A very different attitude indeed from the man who, on first arriving in Danebury saw the women as submissive, dwarf like and almost repulsive to him. The way they bowed and scraped to the men he found quite insulting, both to himself and to them. But Parrish had overcome his prejudice and adapted to the Neolithic way of life and began to understand how the women still managed to eke some enjoyment out of their lives under the stern rule of their men. He understood too that the strict hierarchy of this way of life was necessary for the continuation and integration of the small villages and tribes of Neolithic Britain. The fabric of society was thin and fragile in the land of the young. Disruption of it could mean its destruction.

The Chieftains present appreciation of his wife was two-fold. Even as he gazed at her slim, four foot eleven inch figure and took in her oval face, the long, dark, cascading hair that fell over her shoulders and down her back and the twinkling blue eyes, his own eyes automatically dropped to the very slight bulge of her lower belly. It was barely visible beneath her clothing but he knew it was there and just the thought of it cheered him. Juli had fallen pregnant, almost three moons since, and now carried what he hoped would be his son. Parrish's attitude was still 20th century enough to believe that as long as the baby arrived fit and healthy he did not much mind whether it was a boy or girl, but a son would be a preferable and more welcome offspring for the rest of the village, as befitted a Chieftain.

Juli noticed where her tall husbands gaze rested and saw the joy in his eyes. She would not dare to show any affection toward him in public but she felt an almost overwhelming urge to go to him. She had no word for it, indeed there was no word for it in the language of Neolithic Britain, but knew in her heart that she loved him as much as he loved her and it required a great effort to suppress a return smile. Juli knew Klud's hawk like eyes would see the gesture as an insult and then Parrish would have had to act against it.

The Neolithic man simply dismissed the woman with a passing glance and looked once again to Parrish. The tall man dragged his eyes from his wife and met Klud's gaze, eyebrows going up in question.

"I have come to tell you that the holy man wishes to speak with you."

Parrish nodded.

"Tell him that I will come at once."

"He is at the Chieftains hut."

Klud nodded back and led off down the slope, clearly expecting Parrish to follow.

Parrish turned and fired a quick wink at Juli before setting off after the warrior. After first making sure that Klud's back was still turned, she flashed a quick smile in return then went back into their house.

2

The holy man waited patiently beneath the thatch covered porch of the Chieftains hut. This hut was the one traditionally occupied by the village Chieftain and was identical to all the other family huts in Danebury, apart from the extending front porch and the ornately carved and decorated wooden pillars that supported it.

Before Parrish had become head of Danebury he had already built himself an oblong log cabin on the high ground inside the hillfort. Although the Chieftains hut was his official residence, he chose to live in his own cabin and who were the people to argue on his strange choice. After all, he was Chieftain and his word was final.

For the holy man himself, the only man in Danebury who lived a solitary and celibate lifestyle, home was inside the great hut of the Earth Goddess, behind the all dominating statue of Dannu herself. He was Dannu's voice to the people of the village and their voice to her. To that end, the village kept him without calling on him to do any physical work. All his efforts directed into keeping the village strong were on a spiritual level. The people had the utmost respect for the little man and his close contact with the Earth Goddess. Similarly, the people also felt the same about Parrish, knowing him to be close to the Earth Goddess also. When he was not within earshot he was often referred to as Dannu's man.

Parrish himself was still sceptical of the pagan worship practiced by the people although he had experienced a number of strange, unexplainable happenings which, while not causing him to fully believe in the Earth Goddess, never the less rendered him much more open to and respectful of this ancient and mysterious religion.

Parrish and Klud strode side by side through the village and the holy man watched the two approach. The six foot tall Chieftain towered over all the other occupants of the village yet, apart from his great height, his boots and the camouflage jacket that he sometimes wore, he was more or less indistinguishable in appearance from the other warriors.

The little Neolithic shaman smiled briefly at the man's easy stride and the nods and bows of respect and acknowledgment Parrish received as he passed among his people. It had to be admitted that he had not been treated at all favourably by the holy man during his first days at Danebury, or by anyone else for that matter.

He had simply walked out of Dannu's vast land one day, bringing with him the warm summer sun, unable to speak or even take care of himself. But he was Dannu's man, for he could do things that no mortal man could do. He could find his way unerringly through blizzards or the darkness and sometimes he exchanged strange gifts made from materials never seen before. He could draw the great bow that his friend Mars the archer had made for him. A bow that no one else could pull and that fired the far reaching arrows fletched with the feathers of the sky spirits.

And he was unbeatable in single combat. The holy man had himself seen Parrish kill a man in the blink of an eye, with his bare hands. Yes, he was a special man. The people of Danebury knew this, were honoured to have him walk among them and had happily chosen him as Chieftain when the former Chieftain had been slain in battle. A battle in which Parrish had claimed four heads, by any standards a large number of trophies for a single fight. It was somewhat ironic that part of the reason for his choice as Chieftain, the people's belief that he was Dannu's man, was one that he was completely unaware of.

Parrish considered the waiting shaman as he approached the Chieftains hut. He himself liked the holy man, although he would never say so out loud. He liked him because he saw him as the forerunner of an island tradition, the great British eccentric. The little man did not act, think or live the same way as other people yet was still universally respected and admired for his single minded devotion to the Earth Goddess. By dint of those same religious beliefs of the people this also made him a powerful man in the village. Almost as powerful as the Chieftain, Parrish liked him too because he knew that, if he chose to, he could wield that power and make life very difficult for Danebury's leader and all the rest of the village. Yet he did not. He was a good man and cared for the village as much as the Chieftain did. And finally, Parrish liked him because the religion that he represented required him to wear certain apparel, namely an outrageous hat intertwined with different coloured feathers and forest flowers and a cape that had more of the same woven among its threads. Although he knew that each item he wore was symbolic of the connections between nature, the land and the people, it simply cheered Parrish to see such a brightly clothed individual standing out among the more sombre buckskins and woollens worn by everybody else.

The two warriors nodded and sat down opposite the holy man.

"Greetings Parrish." was all the shaman said as they settled, not needing to rise for the Chieftain, the only man in the camp with that privilege.

"What is it you wish to talk with me about?" asked the Chieftain. The holy man suppressed a smile before answering. It was a typical Parrish start to a conversation. He always had questions, ever since he had first learned to speak. Never before had he met a man who had so many questions.

"It is time."

"Time for what?" It was Parrish's turn to suppress a smile. All the holy men of the land seemed almost to be trained in the art of speaking in riddles, something that before he had learned to accept Parrish found irritating and frustrating. It took a while for him to understand that all that was required to understand the holy ones was patience. Their hidden meanings became clear eventually.

"You have been Chieftain for several moons now. The winter is past, the fields are seeded, the village wall and ditch had been attended to and repaired and the sun again grows warm. The people are now not so busy and so, it is time."

Parrish didn't bother to repeat his question. He just waited. Realizing that he was not going to get a response, the holy man continued, seemingly unconcerned with the Chieftains apparent lack of interest. He knew he would have to explain to the big man. There were still many things about village life and ritual that he did not know.

"Every Chieftain must have his own chamber in the earth, ready and waiting for him when the time comes to return to the arms of the

Earth Goddess. You must take men, chose your place and build your chamber."

Parrish knew that the holy man meant for him to build himself a burial mound and also knew that the burial tombs of the Chieftains were all up on Salisbury Plain.

"I understand. How soon must the job be done?"

"Quite soon. It would be well if the chamber is ready before the long walk, but that is still many moons away yet."

"OK." Parrish nodded. The other two men understood the strange phrase to mean yes. "I will decide on the strength of the work party and let you know my decision. Will you be with us?"

"No. I have selected an apprentice to follow in the footsteps of Dannu. Now he must learn the ways of her worship. The two of us must go to the village of the temple of the Earth Goddess, but I will return for the final approval of your chamber."

Parrish thought back to his own experience of the high priests of the temple and did not envy the boy his journey. At any rate, it would certainly be a journey of discovery to the large causewayed camp on the gently sloping hill behind the great stone circle of Avebury, grand temple to Dannu the Earth Goddess.

"Will you be safe travelling alone or should I send some men with you?"

"We will be safe enough. No one would dare attack a holy one." The little man believed utterly his own words. Parrish was not so sure but, if anyone knew the people of the land, it was the little shaman.

"Very well." He rose to his feet. Understanding that he must now embark on another ritual that was important to the people in his charge, he had already decided to act upon it immediately. "When I have decided on the work party I will have Klud tell the chosen ones, but know now that it is my wish that we go before the next full moon."

That was only six days away and both Klud and the holy man were impressed with the immediacy of the decision. There was of course no doubt that they would go when the Chieftain said, his wish was actually an order, for his word was final. Even so, it was still time enough for the people who would be chosen for the work to get their own houses in order before going off to do the Chieftains bidding. It was a good decision.

With a brief bow of his head Parrish headed off back towards his cabin.

The two Neolithic men watched him go. Klud finally turned to his companion beneath the porch.

"There are many things he still does not know but, once he understands, he immediately seems to do the right thing."

"Yes. Dannu guides him in word and thought." The holy man spoke what they were both thinking. He was impressed with Parrish and his commitment to the people and village of Dane-bre and, although he said no more, allowed a small smile to slip briefly across his usually serious features.

Parrish returned to his cabin. The people of Danebury thought its strange, square construction odd. Some even considered it stupid and very non functional although they no longer said so. Yet they had all gladly assisted in building it, a debt of honour to the tall man. Inside, Juli had taken some meat from the smokehouse behind the cabin and was preparing it for the evening meal. The day was still young and Parrish knew that what she was doing meant that either she had some particularly long task to do next or else she intended everything to be ready early so that they could spend some free time together later.

He entered quietly and crept up behind her before grabbing her swiftly about the waist, making her jump.

"Oh! You frightened me." she gasped.

"Sorry." He laughed and lowered his hands onto her little bump. "I forgot. I must be careful not to frighten the little one too."

Juli smiled. Her husband could be so strange. Why should he apologize to a mere woman or bother so much with something that is not yet born?

Carrying a baby is just one more of a woman's normal duties. Yet she alone knew how proud he was at the coming of his child and, for some strange reason, proud of her too. She didn't understand it but she loved him for it.

If she seriously thought about it, she didn't really understand all that much about her tall husband, but to her that was not important. It was enough that she trusted him utterly, believed in him and was grateful for the wonderful feelings he gave her when they lay together. It did not occur to her that the reason the sensations were so wonderful were because of the feelings she had for him as much as those he had for her. She *did* understand that there had never before been a man like him on Dannu's land. A man who had feelings like him or acted according to them. Of this she was sure.

Many times, when the women gathered at the stream while fetching water, a place where men did not often go, they had spoken together of Parrish's strange ways. It was their considered opinion that the Chieftain was indeed Dannu's man. Given both the power and skills of a great warrior, and also the womanly cares of the Goddess. A man like no other.

Juli turned to face her husband, tilting her head up to see his smiling face. As if holding eye contact with him wasn't a bold enough gesture, she plucked up her courage and used one of the gifts he had given her that was still so strange to her and unusual for a Neolithic woman, that she paused a moment before taking the plunge.

"What was it that the holy man wanted?" There. She had asked him another question.

"To tell me that I must build a chamber up on the Great Plain ready for when I die." Parrish didn't know quite how difficult it was for his wife to speak freely and ask questions. He simply assumed that she always paused before speaking to construct the sentences in her head. "And that it must be done quite soon."

Juli nodded, not enjoying the thought that one day her husband would be dead. Her face never betrayed her feelings.

"Tell me," he asked. "How big are these chambers to be?" Then she smiled. More of his questions.

"They are like the village burial mound only not so big." She glanced around their house. "With only a small chamber inside them to put the body in but the mound over it is as big as this cabin."

Parrish nodded and kissed his wife on the mouth, something else she did not understand but nevertheless enjoyed, then released her from his grip and sat down on the edge of the bed. Juli watched him for a moment then, realizing that he was thinking, left him alone with his thoughts and carried on with her chores. That was how it was when the Chieftain needed to think.

Parrish was indeed thinking. There were many things to consider. He wasn't particularly bothered about where he lay once he was dead. The best that a man can hope for when he is gone is that he lives on in the thoughts and words of others, and so he is not forgotten. To the people of Danebury though it was an important part of their culture and their way of honouring the dead, especially their Chieftains. Juli had confirmed his own ideas concerning a burial chamber. He had been inside the village long barrow but its central, stone lined chamber was easily as big as his cabin. It needed to be because it held the main bones of all the people who had ever been born, lived and died in Danebury. He had also led his people up onto the Great Plain in his capacity as new Chieftain to entomb the body of the man who he replaced.

Chieftain Coran had been a brave man, a wise man and a good friend.

When he had been laid to rest, to lie in patient wait for the Earth Goddess, Parrish had foolishly paid very little attention to Coran's burial mound, just remembering it as an irregular hump in the ground. The final farewell ceremony had taken place outside and only the holy man and the pall bearers had actually entered his tomb.

And now he must build one of his own. To all intents and purposes he must dig his own grave. Needless to say, Parrish was not exactly thrilled with the prospect, but it was required. He applied himself to the task.

The construction of the central stone chamber and its approach tunnel would need some skill and expertise but he was sure that the village had that. How else would they have constructed all the other past Chieftains tombs? The rest of the job was simply a case of moving a volume of earth, a basic matter of tools and manpower.

He eventually decided to take twenty men with him. That would still leave a little more than twenty able bodied men to look after the crops, the sheep and to protect the village, yet still give him enough strong backs to get his job done quickly. A speedily completed job meant a quicker return to the safety of the village to bring it back again to full strength. He would also ban hunting during the time he was away. The village defences would be depleted enough during his absence without hunting parties irresponsibly disappearing off into the great forest for days at a time.

Klud would surely know who among the warriors were the stonemason's, while Parrish himself would select the rest of the work party. With at least one wife per man as well as camp equipment, food and tools, he would be leading a sizable group up onto the Plain. Perhaps then it might be a good idea if he first tried the southern edge of the area to look for his chosen place. After all, it was not as far to go and safer than just swanning out onto the open Plain where the protection of cover was virtually non-existent.

Yes, he would keep his group at the edge of the forest where they could pull quickly back under its protective canopy if danger threatened. Either way, they would camp there during the nights.

"Juli." he said finally, rising from the bed. "I am going to see Klud. The work party needs to be chosen. I have decided that we will go just before the next full moon, so be ready."

Juli just nodded. She didn't understand why he needed to tell her what he had decided. The women were expected to always be ready and a man never explained his actions or intentions to a woman. She gave the only answer a woman can give to a warrior.

"Yes."

3

Parrish led his entourage, all of forty five persons strong, away from Danebury early in the morning. All the men were well armed, both for hunting as well as for protection, and the women were loaded down with supplies, camping and building equipment. Admittedly the building tools were just shoulder blade shovels, antler picks and polished stone hammers but Parrish still considered the distribution of load grossly unfair. He never said anything, knowing from experience that the price of equality could be high if the group were unlucky enough to be attacked while the men had their hands full.

Parrish had walked around and checked the encampment the previous night, ensuring all was well and that the remaining warriors knew their stations and their duties. He had put a man of stout character and sound judgment in temporary command of the hillfort.

Gant, he of the bear attack and forever in debt to the Chieftain, had been honoured to accept the appointment. The warrior had helped to build the tall stranger's cabin and Parrish recalled how quickly the man had grasped the basic concept of productive organization. A good choice. He smiled at the recollection of how he had also needed to pacify and console his young friend Tomps on telling the lad that he would not be going with the burial mound work party.

Tomps was only fifteen summers old but already had a wife, a girl he had bartered for from another village, and three heads to his credit. He was the youngest warrior in Danebury to have his own stall in the shrine hut of the Earth Goddess. He had also been Parrish's first contact in the Neolithic world and since become very close to the tall man. His position was such that he was good friend, *senior* hunting partner too and learner of knowledge from the Chieftain of his village. A rare, even unique claim for one so young, anywhere in the known lands. Yet he was still only a boy in stature and for the task ahead Parrish needed strong backs.

With Gant's prior consent, he had pacified the young man with the position of second in command. In itself the post meant nothing because the man in charge was like the Chieftain and as such his say was final, but when told, Tomps proudly puffed out his chest. Tomps was also good friend to Klud and for him to hold a position beside Gant, like the one Klud held beside Parrish, was a matter of great pride, no matter that it was only a temporary position.

Next, Parrish had ensured that the holy man and the small boy he had chosen, a lad that the Chieftain did not know personally, were fully equipped and ready for their own journey. He had watched them leave ahead of his own party, marvelling at the sheer balls of a single, defenceless little man walking with impunity through the dangerous lands of Neolithic southern England. The holy man never gave his own actions any consideration. He simply thought that soon, once word of the tall man's deeds had spread, the people would realize that Parrish was Dannu's man and then he also could walk her land without fear.

The Chieftain and his band, once they had left the safe confines of the village, travelled slowly but steadily across the rolling landscape on an almost due east heading, according to Parrish's well concealed but regularly checked survival compass. They were on their way to the southern edge of Salisbury Plain, where it dipped down to meet the river Wylye. It was a route that Parrish well remembered from the days when he had first arrived here.

They passed by the excavated site of the flint mines where the old master knapper of Danebury came occasionally with a troop of boys and dug out the lumpy flint nodules. Along most of the chalk downlands of southern England flint could be picked up in large quantities straight off the ground, but it was invariably light brown in colour and of poor quality. The very high quality black, glassy looking flint that lay hidden under its white coating of cortex needed to be dug out of the earth, sometimes from as much as six to eight feet below ground level. This was the raw material of the knappers trade and after mining was laboriously carried back to the hillfort in wicker baskets.

Just a few kilometres beyond the mines in the direction of the setting sun, a river flowing southwards cut through the fertile green landscape. Only Parrish knew the river as the Avon. Once across it the rest of the party would be in unknown territory and relying solely on their Chieftains mysteriously acquired knowledge of the area.

All of Danebury's hunting parties went either north or east from the hillfort into the great forest and the annual trip to the great temple of Dannu led off to the north-west. No one from the village had ever travelled beyond the natural, western boundary of the river. Only Parrish knew that he and his group were fording the river just a few kilometres north of where the Avon, the Wylye and the Nadder all converged. The rivers met now in what was just an open expanse of low laying meadows, but one day the place would boast a magnificent cathedral crowned with the highest spire in Britain, Salisbury.

As they prepared to cross, Klud pointed downstream to a prominent hill not half a kilometre distant.

"That would be a good hill to build a fort on." he said.

"Yes." agreed Parrish, recognizing the hill in question. "You could be right."

Are right, he thought, eyeing the as yet still untouched mound of Sarum. It would indeed become a hillfort but not for another two thousand years yet.

The party crossed the river without incident and continued on its way, up and over the partially wooded ridge between the paths of the Avon and the Wylye, then on down towards the second sparkling ribbon of water ahead of them. That was where Parrish had decided to camp for the night. There was still several hours of daylight left and his decision surprised most of the warriors. They were all for carrying on, but never said.

As they reached the riverbank Parrish announced that here there was fresh water, nearby shelter and a chance of fresh meat and so it would be a good place to stop. It was true enough but Parrish also had an ulterior motive. He wanted to go back up onto the ridge and see if he could find his original camp site. The place where he had spent his very first night in the land of the young. He knew in his heart that there was very little chance of him finding anything at all but it was a trip down memory lane and so, when the camp was settled, he returned to the high ground alone. It seemed to the other members of the party that he simply paced about under the trees until it was almost too dark to see. None of them questioned his actions. They did think it strange but assumed he was in some way communicating with the Earth Goddess. Even Juli kept silent when he finally returned to the camp and sat beside the fire, eating in thoughtful silence.

The next morning Parrish told the people under his charge that he had decided to cross this river too. He knew they weren't very happy about the seemingly regular dunkings but didn't hear anyone complain.

Beyond the far bank another ridge rose up before them, much higher than the last one. It stretched away to the west and was paralleled by rivers on both its north and south flanks, to the north by the Wylye and the south by the Nadder. Parrish chose to follow the south river. True, it was at the very southernmost limit of the Salisbury Plain area yet still within the boundary for Chieftains burial mounds, as designated by the holy men who required the chamber to be on higher ground. The north river Parrish discounted because he had followed its course once before, albeit in the opposite direction, from the site of the accident that had hurled him back in time. He discounted it because his trip the previous night up to his old camp site had only succeeded in bringing back to him memories of the 20th century and all the things he missed there. It was unexpectedly painful to recall his parents, friends and all the people and places he would never see again. He didn't fancy anymore unnecessary trips down memory lane thank you very much!

The work party waded their way through the refreshing, if somewhat chill water then started traversing along the lower slopes of the south side of the ridge, keeping the river quite close on their left and the partially wooded high ground to the right. It was warm and pleasant enough, clothing dried quickly and the people moved along at an easy, strength conserving pace. Now Parrish had two warriors scouting ahead on point and another three strung out in a line in the trees above. He had no intention of being caught out by a surprise attack. There was little fear of any immediate threat from the direction of the river but he kept an eye out in that quarter anyway.

Summer was indeed well on its way. By the time the sun was high in the clear blue sky the temperature was well up in the natural sun trap of the Nadder valley. Eventually coming to a small tributary of the river, Parrish called a stop for rest and water. It was quite a picturesque place, located as it was in its own small, shallow valley that had been slowly cut into the land by the constant flow of the stream and its gradual erosion of the soft, rich topsoil. A peaceful little haven then, nestling below the sweeping slopes of the great ridge. Indeed, early Saxon people would one day site their little village alongside the stream. The modern map marked the place as Teffont Magna, still considered a beauty spot even in the 20th century.

Juli offered her husband some cuts of smoked meat and a water bag then sat down close beside him. Before she could speak Klud's shadow fell across them. He sat down uninvited on the Chieftains opposite side, ignoring her.

"This place is not known to us, Parrish." he said flatly. "Even the long distance hunting parties do not travel this way." Parrish nodded as he finished his mouthful and washed it down with a draught of water. The hunting parties frowned on hunting over open ground.

They also seemed somehow to know that in the sandy, gravelly and much more sparsely wooded area of the Hampshire Basin game was less plentiful than beneath the forest canopy. Hunting parties did not come west so of course they did not know the land here. However, Parrish certainly knew the area from the countless training exercises he had endured during eight years in the Light Infantry. He did not want the work party to start getting unnecessarily nervous. Now was a good time to announce his intentions.

"Do not worry." he said finally. "Soon I shall pick a spot and there we shall build. Tell the others this if you like." Klud nodded, pleased that the Chieftain had understood his hidden meaning, rose swiftly to his feet and left the couple without another word.

Juli leaned in closer and whispered to her husband.

"Why do you come this way? Is not the great Plain on the way to Dannu's temple?"

She pointed off to the north. Parrish pulled her hand down with his and gave it a tender squeeze.

"I know, but that way is also the place where I first arrived here. It is not a place that I wish to visit again."

"Oh. I see." She didn't and Parrish knew it. He laughed.

"It is of no matter to you, my wife. Soon we shall build my chamber and them we can all return to the safety of Dane-bre. Do not be afraid."

She looked about to make sure that no one was watching, then gave her husband a quick but heartfelt hug.

"I am not afraid. I know I am safe as long as I am with you."

He gave her a warm smile and gently patted her lower abdomen. She clasped his hand to her body.

"I know we are both safe." she said, seeing the pleasure in his eyes that her pregnant condition somehow gave him. Parrish looked down at her almost invisible roundness beneath his palm and smiled to himself.

"My mum would have been chuffed to bits." he said softly in English.

Juli didn't understand her husband's strange, unintelligible words and had given up asking him what they meant. If she had asked him to change them into words she knew, they would almost certainly have still made little sense to her. Parrish too had long since realized that the meanings of most English words were somehow lost in translation. Juli just marvelled at how her husband could understand the nonsense sounds that he spoke to himself when he was in the strange, deep thinking, almost mystic mood that overtook him sometimes. Yes, there were strange forces at work around her husband.

The two were jarred from their individual thoughts by someone calling out for the Chieftain. Parrish immediately jumped to his feet and, ignoring all the looks of sudden curiosity and concern on the faces of everyone around him, went to the man who had called out, meeting him halfway across the little encampment. The eagle eyed warrior Narn pointed urgently towards the ridge. Emerging hurriedly from the lower tree line were the scouts Parrish had positioned on the high ground.

He waited patiently as the three men entered the gathering at the run, making a bee line towards him. By the time the scouts had reached their Chieftain all the rest of the party were on their feet.

The men stopped, panting, before Parrish. As one they opened their mouths to speak but he stopped them with a single, raised hand.

"I know." was all he said, looking over their heads and up to the distant skyline of the ridge, no more than two kilometres distant. Everyone spun, following his line of sight with their own eyes.

Coming over the brow, moving slowly in single file and heading straight for the little Danebury camp, were a band of unknown warriors!

4

By the time the unknown band of men emerged from the trees into the afternoon sunshine the people of Danebury were ready and waiting, formed into a tight, defensive line. The warriors were poised, weapons at the ready. The women huddled together behind their men for safety. Parrish commanded his men from the centre of the line, trying to appear totally calm and utterly fearless for their benefit. He in fact felt the opposite and was envious of his charges, knowing there was no fear among the Neolithic men standing beside him. Fear wasn't in their mental vocabulary, their faces just showing grim determination.

The mystery group were somehow unaware of the close proximity of the Danebury group and only spotted them once they had emerged from the tree line. They jerked to a surprised halt, immediately huddling close together for defence and readying their own weapons. Two men had to shrug deer carcasses from their shoulders to do this. It was a hunting party from some unknown village and Parrish counted only ten men.

The smaller party stared at the much larger group and they in turn stared back. A Mexican standoff. Parrish knew as well as everyone else that the first to lower his gaze and back away would be dishonoured and suffer loss of face. He also knew that that would not happen. As if to confirm his thoughts Klud spoke quietly out of the corner of his mouth, not taking his eyes from the hunting party opposite.

"There will be a battle." he said, attempting to put his Chieftain in the picture, knowing that his tall friend had never been in a situation like this and might not be ready for what was about to happen. "They must attack but we are many more. At least they will die with honour." he added grudgingly.

Parrish thought fast. He had no doubt the ten men would die but that was not his main concern. He was cooling calculating how many of his own people might die in the apparently imminent and seemingly unavoidable conflict.

"Not if I can help it." he said finally and stepped forward from the line, much to the amazement of his warriors.

There were gasps from the women behind the line and a heightening of tension from both the men a step behind him and the group out ahead. Parrish carefully laid his great longbow on the ground and took a few more steps forward, aware and grateful that his men were covering him. He extended his arms, hands open and called clearly across the open ground between himself and the little band.

"I would speak with your leader."

There was a prolonged moment of tense silence, then a whispered conversation among the small group. At length Parrish saw several nods before a man finally stepped clear of the huddle. He handed his own bow to one of his colleagues and, resting one hand almost too casually on the war club tucked into his tunic belt, started on a slow walk towards the tall man.

Parrish started forward, matching him step for step. The tension in both watching groups was now almost tangible.

The two men at the centre of everyone's attention came together at the middle of the clearing, stopping several paces short of one another. Parrish looked down at the leader of the mysterious hunting party. Of medium Neolithic build and about five foot one in height, he had a striking ginger beard in relation to the rest of the hair on his head, which was very dark. The smaller man looked unwaveringly up into Parrish's face for a long moment before acknowledging him with a barely perceptible nod of the head. He received a return nod of similar proportions.

"You are the tall one called Parrish." he said suddenly.

Parrish was a bit taken aback by the recognition. At first all he could do was nod in acknowledgment before recovering his surprise and drawing himself up to his full height.

"It is true, but I do not know your name."

"I am Tanis of Amaldach-bre." the bearded man replied proudly.

The name meant nothing to Parrish even though he now fully understood the Gaelic/Celtic dialect the people of the times spoke. He understood 'bre' to mean hill and 'amaldach' to mean either obstacle or hindrance.

In fact the village of Tanis and his band *was* called such because it's surrounding defences and the lie of the immediately surrounding land made it a severe obstacle or hindrance to approach.

In true Gaelic the word - AMALADACH means hindrance. Tanis pronounced it 'Amaldach' and over the passing centuries the word would gradually and subtly change into what it now is in modern English.

Amaldach-bre to Hambledon Hill.

Parrish could see that the man took great pride in his association with his village, quite rightly so, and decided to out pride the man there and then and stamp his own authority over the proceedings.

"And I am Parrish, Chieftain of Dane-bre." His voice was forceful.

This sudden revelation visibly shocked Tanis and he took an involuntary step back, his natural respect for a Chieftain struggling against his right of challenge to another warrior. Either way, proper respect must be paid and he bowed more deeply this time to the tall man.

"Greetings, Chieftain Parrish." he said. There could of course be no apology for his effrontery at talking to a Chieftain as an equal, but it at the very least required an explanation. "I thought Coran to be head of Dane-bre village."

"He died with great honour this autumn gone. Now I am Chieftain." Tanis bowed again. Parrish paused before continuing.

"In a few moments there will be blood spilled here." He waited to see if there would be any comment from the red bearded man. There was none. Tanis only thought that the tall stranger was simply stating the obvious. He returned the man's steady gaze, waiting for the Chieftains next words.

"It is not necessary. If you attack us you will all die. It does not matter to me if you die, but my people are here to help me build my chamber. This is the wish of the Earth Goddess. I do not want to carry out her task with my hands wet with men's blood."

Tanis did not know very much about the tall man opposite him but could plainly see that he was different from all other men who walked Dannu's land. He noticed also the fletching of the arrows in the quiver slung across the giants back.

Fletching made from the feathers of the sacred sky spirits. And then realization dawned as he recalled the rumours. Stories that had been passed about after the last time of trading at the 'gathering point', near the Great Temple of the Earth Goddess. Tanis paid little attention to the seemingly tall tales bandied about by the women and weak minded men of his village. Those stories that told of a tall stranger. Of one who was thought to be Dannu's man. Yet here, face to face with the tall one, it somehow seemed that the tales now had a ring of truth.

For the first time too he was suddenly aware that, although just moments before he had readied himself to go to battle and suffer possible defeat, he was now truly looking into the face of death.

At that moment, as he looked up into those hard, piercing eyes and realised just who stood before him, a cold feeling of inevitability swept over him. Dannu was close, he sensed her, and he somehow knew he had no defence against the tall man. Rocking him almost like a physical blow, he all at once inescapably knew that this tall, powerful man was the one. The one who, sooner or later, would end his time upon the land of the Earth Goddess. It took all his willpower to stop from taking more steps back away from his nemesis. Unaware of the chilling insight that Tanis had just received, Parrish spoke again.

"If you give me your word of honour that you will not attack us, I will stay the hands of my warriors and allow you safe passage."

It was a skilfully phrased question. Parrish seemed at first to be doing the unthinkable as a warrior and offering to back down, yet by exercising his right as Chieftain and not allowing his vastly superior force to have its way and take the smaller bands heads as trophies, he was offering Tanis and his men an honourable exit from the no win situation they now found themselves in. Tanis did not understand all this, except for the last part, but he had his honour too and could not be seen to back down without some show of defiance.

"I will give you my word." he said, after much thought, "But my warriors need to rest before travelling on. We had planned to spend the night here. If you in turn give me your word of honour that your warriors will not attack us, we will camp further downstream and be on our way at the rise of sun tomorrow."

Parrish understood. With honours exchanged and boldness

displayed by Tanis and his men, even at a distance, both groups could continue about their business without loss of face and, more importantly to Parrish, without loss of life.

He bowed slightly to the Neolithic warrior in agreement. Tanis had to bow deeper as Parrish was a Chieftain but that was expected and not taken as submission. The two backed away from each other for a few paces then turned and returned to their own groups.

There was astonishment in both camps as the arrangement was announced. The Danebury warriors were understandably upset that they had been robbed of a chance for trophies but when Parrish explained that spilling blood while fulfilling a task for Dannu was not showing proper respect, they saw the wisdom of his words and agreed.

The Hambledon Hill warriors were silently glad that they need not die after all and were amazed at the strange truce arranged by who they now realised was the one rumour spoke of as Dannu's man. On hearing how Tanis had also arranged for them to camp daringly near to a much greater force without fear because the tall one had pledged that his warriors would not attack, they praised him for it. He was truly a great leader for standing in defiance of such a warrior. A tale indeed to tell back at Amaldach-bre. It would much enhance their standing as warriors in their village.

The remainder of the afternoon passed under a strain. The warriors from Hambledon Hill had moved less than half a kilometre downstream. Only four hundred meters away and deliberately visible, they were clearly thumbing their noses at a much greater force. The Danebury group had formed itself into a circle of men while the women attended cooking fires within it. Parrish and his people cast constant glances at the little camp just a short way away and were well aware of the constant eyes on them too.

As the evening drew on and the light began to fade Parrish put two men on sentry duty twenty meters or so out from the camp perimeter, with somewhat superfluous orders to keep their eyes and ears peeled once darkness had descended. He could clearly see that the opposite camp had also done similarly, although he doubted that they would know he had also arranged stags throughout the night so his people would benefit from constantly fresh and alert lookouts. The morning would find all Danebury's warriors rested and refreshed. Tiredness could be dangerous.

A group of the women, Juli included, made their way down to the babbling waters to wash out the rough clay cooking pots and their other pieces of crockery. It was some distance from the campsite to the stream because camping too close to the water invited constant harassment from the hordes of midges that bred at the water's edge.

The women were in the process of cleaning their wares when the sound of approaching footsteps in the dusk alerted them. Before they could gather up the pots and retreat to the safety of their own camp three men approached.

Men they did not recognize!

The men, led by Tanis, were genuinely not out for mischief, simply hoping for a chance to collar the women into cleaning their own pots which they carried, and fill their water bags from the unsullied water in mid stream. They had no desire to do their own cleaning up or get unnecessarily wet. That was woman's work and why should they not take advantage when there were women about to do it? It mattered not that they were from some other village, women were still duty bound to obey men. All men.

Juli and the others looked longingly over their shoulders at the safety of their own camp, almost a hundred metres away. It might as well have been a hundred kilometres. Now the three strangers were within speaking distance the women had to obey their commands.

Tanis and his two warriors dropped their pots and skin bags at the feet of the women.

"Clean and fill these." said the red bearded man arrogantly.

With undisguised looks of fear on their faces the women put down their own goods and bent to pick up the warrior's pots. The men stepped back and looked on, arms folded over puffed out chests.

Juli was slower to react to the order than the other women, reluctant to release her grip on the pots she was holding. Her reluctance was immediately spotted by Tanis and he rounded on the small woman.

"What is this?! Did you not hear me? I said ..." He stopped as his eyes settled on two of the items Juli clutched to her chest, different from all the other clay pots. Of an unusual shape, they almost glistened in the half light. A sudden sense of dread filled Juli as she realised that he had spotted her husband's strange, square shaped pots. Parrish always referred to them as 'mess tins'. They were made from the mysterious, odd feeling material he called 'metal' and he had often told her that metal was very, very rare here.

Clearly, and not surprisingly, the objects interested Tanis.

"Let me see them."

Juli was once again slow to react and the Neolithic warrior assumed that the girl was simply stupid, even for a female, and unaware that she was trying to protect her husband's property.

"Give them to me!" He barked, beginning to get angry.

Before Juli could stop herself she heard the single, unforgivable word fall from her mouth.

"No."

The other women gasped.

Tanis immediately became enraged at being so boldly and openly insulted by a woman. He grabbed Juli savagely by the arm and hauled her roughly towards him, raising his free hand in a clenched fist.

In the Danebury camp the sounds of women screaming in fear galvanized the warriors to arms. Snatching up the nearest weapons they raced towards the stream in a close group, ready for anything, Parrish at its head.

At the water's edge the women cowered away to one side while the Hambledon Hill men looked on. Juli lay beaten and bleeding on the ground between the two. Before the running warriors arrived Tanis had completed his punishment of Juli, landing several telling blows to her face and body then kicking her a number of times once she had fallen to the ground. Seeing the state of his wife, Parrish let out an enraged cry and leapt for Tanis, only to find himself being held back by a number of his own warriors.

"It is only a woman." said Klud quickly. "We cannot go to battle over a mere female." He leaned in closer to his furious Chieftain. "And you have given your word." he hissed.

All Parrish did in reply was hiss back through gritted teeth but he stopped struggling against the restraining arms, letting his own go limp at his sides. He fixed Tanis with a stare that made the Neolithic man wince. The Hambledon Hill man didn't understand what was going on. As far as he was concerned he had done no wrong.

A Danebury warrior spoke quickly with one of the women then stood before his Chieftain. It was all Parrish could do to drag his burning stare from Tanis to look down at the other man.

"She says your wife refused to obey the warrior and then openly denied him. It is a great insult my Chieftain and he was right to punish her."

For a moment Parrish stared in disbelief at the man before understanding dawned as to what had just happened here. Even though he didn't like it one bit he recognized it as the truth as these Stone Age men saw it and knew they all thought Tanis had acted correctly. He glanced at Klud who nodded as if in agreement. The anger still burned inside Parrish but now he controlled it. It would of course be unacceptable to his men if he attacked the man who had attacked his little wife. The breath he held exploded from his lungs, he clenched and unclenched his fists then shrugged free of the arms that held him. Ignoring everyone else he went straight to his wife and knelt beside her. He scooped Juli gently up into his arms, making her groan with pain, and without a single word or backward glance at the rest of the men, set off back to camp. The other women followed close behind the tall man. After a few well directed hard stares, the warriors of Danebury also followed their leader away.

The last man to leave the three Hambledon Hill men was Klud, who turned his full attention on Tanis. The red bearded man was still baffled by what had just happened, staring in disbelief at the all apparent fury that had been on the tall man's face and the tender, almost respectful way he had acted towards his woman. Klud fixed him with a cold stare, knowing what he was thinking, and spoke, his voice quiet and low.

"No one knows why he acts towards his wife as he does," was all he offered by way of an explanation. "But know this." He pointed an accusing finger at Tanis. "You will never be closer to death than you have just been. Not until the time when Dannu comes for you!"

Then, blatantly exposing his unguarded back to the three warriors, Klud turned and walked slowly away from the astounded, staring men.

Parrish tried to assist the women who were tending to his battered wife but they had control of the situation and all he did was keep getting in the way. He couldn't help it, his heart cried for his poor wife.

One of her eyes was already starting to close, blood trickled from the corner of her mouth where the lip was split and she appeared to have bruised, perhaps even cracked ribs. He could barely contain the anger that raged inside him and he stamped up and down beside the central fire, watched with puzzlement by all his warriors. When he went to check on Juli for the umpteenth time Klud's wife, who was in attendance, laid a hand gently on his arm and spoke quietly so that no one else might hear.

"She has been badly beaten my Chieftain, but that is sometimes how it is. She will soon be healed again. Do not worry, we will take care of her."

Parish was grateful to the woman for her kind words but could not bring himself to offer even the smallest smile. He was still consumed with anger at Tanis and concern for his wife.

"Try and rest." Her soft voice urged. "We will look after your wife."

Parrish was finally about to answer Klud's wife when Juli started to moan afresh and clutched at her stomach. A worried look flashed across the woman's face but she quashed it immediately, hoping the Chieftain had not seen it.

"This is woman's work, Parrish." she said urgently. "If something happens I will send word to you. You must get some rest."

It was very bold of her to speak to a warrior in such a manner but she knew that Parrish would not take her well meant words as an insult. That however was not her main concern for she also knew what was now going to happen to Juli and wanted to get Parrish away.

The man who she secretly cared for and was proud to call her Chieftain finally nodded and, with one last anxious glance down at the prostrate figure of his wife, returned to the glare of the fire.

All Parrish could do was listen in anguish to the occasional low moan from his wife and stare into the dancing yellow flames as worry gnawed at his insides and anger burned in his chest.

The night drew on. Men slept, the fire burned lower and the guards continued their regular changes, all things that went on totally unnoticed by the pre-occupied Chieftain of Dane-bre.

Then, sometime in the small hours of the morning, Juli's groans turned to sad sobs. Parrish immediately went to her, arriving just as one of the women was disappearing into the night with a little cloth wrapped bundle held gently in the palms of her cupped hands.

"What was that?" he asked, all at once realizing that he did not want to know the answer. Juli reached up for him and he knelt down beside her, holding onto her hand. She grasped his tighter than ever before, as if she never wanted to let go. Tears rolled unchecked down her bruised face.

"Oh Parrish, ... my husband ... I am so sorry ... " she sobbed, her pain momentarily forgotten.

Klud's first wife knelt beside Parrish and looked into his eyes. It would not normally be permitted but she knew it was necessary.

"I am sorry my Chieftain." Her voice was as soft as it could be. "The baby is gone."

There was a dreadful silence. "There was nothing to be done. It was just not his time. Perhaps ..."

"His? He?" asked Parrish softly. "My son?"

"Yes" was all she could say. The hurt in the tall man's eyes made her want to cry.

"Dead." Parrish's' voice was still quiet but it went flat and hard. A cold rage had come into his chest. So solid did it feel that it almost threatened to choke him.

It became hard for him to breathe. He could no longer think. All he could see was the pathetic little bundle of cloth and the smirking faces of Tanis and his men.

As Klud's wife watched her Chieftains face she saw a part of the man die along with his unborn son. Then, close behind the terrible pain, came a look into his eyes that suddenly frightened her, chilling her to the core. He rose slowly to his feet, letting go of Juli's clutching hand. She reached up for him, both arms outstretched now, but he didn't seem to notice or even hear her cries.

"Parrish ... please, Parrish ... I am so sorry ..." Juli's pitiful pleading fell on deaf ears.

He turned away from her and walked slowly off into the darkness beyond the circle of light thrown by the fire. A hush had fallen over the entire camp and everyone watched as the Chieftain walked off into the night, the only sounds the sobbing of his distraught wife. In a few moments he was gone from sight.

A short time later, out beyond the circle of the camp and the light of the fire, Klud and Narn were doing their stag as lookouts. It was a black, cloudy night with no stars and as Narn was walking the other side of the camp Klud should have been all alone in the dark. But wasn't. He suddenly sensed someone, or something, nearby in the darkness. There was no movement or noise that he could detect but something was out there. And close by. He couldn't explain how he knew, but just knew. There was great danger near at hand. He gripped his flint axe tightly, held it out in readiness before him and said boldly.

"Show yourself. I am Klud of Dane-bre and I will kill you if you do not step forward!"

There was a tense, drawn out silence and the warrior stared intently at the blackness, trying to see beyond the limit of his vision. Then the dark night seemed almost to part like black curtains and a shape swirled before the warrior, its edges blurring together until Klud recognized it as Parrish who stood before him. But not the Parrish Klud knew and was proud to call his friend.

The body was the same, muscular and scarred, although it was stripped to the waist and smeared with black mud that blurred the outline against the dark night and made it difficult to see clearly. And he clutched in one muddy fist the instantly recognizable black bladed metal knife he had carried with him when he had walked out of Dannu's land that day. These things were the same.

But it was the eyes. The pain and anger there made them burn like hot embers. Klud couldn't understand how he could have missed such bright objects in so dark a night.

"Go back to the camp." Parrish's' words came out in short bursts, each one spoken as if it was painful to produce and spit out. "Stay near the fire."

"But the guard ..."

"Go!" was the curt reply and then Parrish moved silently back into the dark until he was once again invisible, swallowed up by the night.

Klud was still staring into the impenetrable darkness when Narn walked up and stood beside him.

"Who were you speaking to?" He asked. "I heard voices."

"We are to go back to the camp." Klud turned and set off towards the suddenly very welcome looking fire. "The Chieftain has ordered it."

"You saw him?" quizzed Narn as he fell in alongside.

"Yes, and I saw more. The fury of Dannu is in our Chieftain. We must go back to the camp where it is safe. Death walks the land this night." Narn nodded although he didn't understand.

Klud stole one last look over his shoulder into the dark night. He was remembering those long moments before Parrish had shown himself. When he had known that something stalked him in the night. Something cold and deadly and without pity. In those moments Klud had experienced something he had never felt before.

He had been afraid.

5

When dawn broke and the sun started to creep its way up over the tree lined horizon, its warm light fell upon the land, including the two separate warrior camps. Both were still, but for vastly different reasons. The Danebury warriors stirred into wakefulness fully expecting to find the camp already moving, with women bustling about and freshly made campfires lit. Yet strangely it was not and the men woke to find the cooking fires cold and their wives huddled close by them for protection, afraid to go out beyond the boundary of the camp for either firewood or water, because of the events of the previous day.

The next unusual thing to be noticed was the complete absence of the sentries. Who should have been on guard at the rise of sun? There was a lot of jostling and elbow nudging of sleepy headed men until everyone in the camp was awake and aware that something was wrong.

Klud had kept his own council through the night and all the other men found him now sitting quiet and still beside central the fire, apparently deep in thought. Rather than simply to send their seemingly disrespectful women straight out into what unexplainably felt like a suddenly very dangerous landscape, the warriors gathered at Klud's side to ask his advice as the Chieftains right hand man. The Chieftain himself suddenly seemed to be absent from his people. The man now at the centre of their attention seemed for a moment to be indifferent to their nearness, staring out into the low sunshine.

"Where are the lookouts?" It was Narn, self elected spokesman for all the others. "And why are the women not busy? What is happening, Klud?"

"I do not know." came the slow reply, Klud not looking at any of the men but continuing to stare out across the land. "But I think that *he* does."

All the warrior did was nod in the direction he was looking and every other head in the camp turned to follow Klud's stare.

Sitting motionless near the edge of the stream, very close to the spot where his wife had been attacked the evening before, was the Chieftain. Many had to squint against the sunlight that reflected off the gently flowing water and seemed to surround Parrish with a bright, flickering glow. He seemed to be simply staring into the bright light but it was difficult to be sure as his back was turned. Beside him on the grass was an irregular, round shaped object, unidentifiable at this distance.

"And there is no movement from the other camp." Klud added after a few moments.

All heads turned to look down along the line of the stream towards the smaller campsite. He was right. All the men from Hambledon Hill seemed to be still tucked snugly up in their bedding, their fire untended and burned away to nothing. All that is except their lone sentry. He was still at his position some twenty meters forward of the camp, but he too lay motionless on the ground. At first it was only Nam and a few other sharp eyed men who spotted him, a low shadow in the grass. He was immediately pointed out to the others. Behind the Danebury warriors the wives also craned their necks to see, listening in silence but with great interest to the men's words.

"What has happened?" Narn changed his question slightly. "I know they have no women but it is wrong to sleep so late."

"Yes." agreed Klud, with more than a hint of tenseness in his voice. He finally looked up at those gathered around him. "Something has happened and I think the Chieftain knows about it." He took a deep breath. "I am going to ask him."

Rising to his feet, he set off towards his friend, the other Danebury men only a step behind. Right behind them came all the women, apart from Klud's first wife who was still tending to a tired but recovering Juli.

It wasn't until Klud was only a few paces from his Chieftain that he finally identified the object laying on the ground beside Parrish. Recognized it would be a better word. He stopped in his tracks, standing very still behind the seated tall man, and gazed down for a long moment with a mixture if admiration and confusion at the severed, red bearded head of Tanis! The long hair was matted with blood and blank eyes stared out into nothingness.

There were jumbled murmurs from the men behind. It was well known that while the Chieftain was happy enough to have his trophies displayed for all to see in his stall, he had always flatly refused to collect them himself. Klud saw his Chieftains bare, mud streaked back tense at the sound of the voices.

"What has happened here?" Klud was nothing if not a man of his word, even if it was not the done thing to ask a Chieftain to explain himself.

Parrish rose slowly to his feet, his metal bladed knife suddenly visible, thrust as it was into the ground beside the severed head.

"I have done a bad thing." he said slowly and turned to face his gathered people. There were several gasps.

His hands and arms were plastered with large amounts of dried blood. Splashes of it, hardened and encrusted where it had dried, spotted his chest and face. Small coagulated lumps dotted his beard, eyebrows and hair. Only Klud saw the look of anguish and shame in his friend's eyes before it was quickly masked with an expression of simple, grim resignation at what he had done.

"The men from Amaldach-bre?" It was barely a question for Klud already knew the answer. He has seen the demon in the night.

Parrish simply nodded.

"Help the Chieftain get clean." Klud immediately took charge and instructed the women. "I am going to the other camp." Several wives immediately bustled forward and gently guided their unresisting leader towards the stream. He waded silently in and the women followed, some pulling off their woollen bodices and starting to sponge him down, unconcerned with their own nakedness.

"Wait!" Narn urged Klud, ignoring the women. "We will get our weapons."

"You will not need them." The certainty in Klud's voice stopped the men in their tracks and as one they turned in puzzlement to follow the warrior, already striding steadily off towards the silent gathering of prostrate men, only a short distance away.

The first man they came to was the sentry. He lay where he had died, face down, showing the bloody yet surprisingly neat looking stab wound to his lower back. A more observant eye would have also seen the harsh bruising around the man's mouth where a hand had clamped violently over it. Only looking down on the poor unfortunate for a few moments, the mystified entourage moved on to the main camp.

All the men there did indeed still lay in their beds but they did not sleep. Nor would they ever wake. As the warriors of Danebury passed dumbly among them, examining each body in turn, it soon became apparent that all their throats had been cut. All that is except for Tanis, whose head lay on the stream bank some four hundred meters away, hacked roughly off by a sharp bladed knife.

"They are all dead." said someone rather unnecessarily. "Killed whilst they slept." No one needed to say that it was not an honourable way to die.

"But how?" asked another. "Did not a single one of them hear anything and wake? What about the lookout, surely he was not asleep?"

"It was done without sound." decided Nam. "And I cannot see how they were approached. There are no tracks."

The last statement wasn't exactly true but as the men of Danebury had already walked through the camp it would have been difficult to spot any individual footprints anyway. Even so, as each man gazed intently down at the ground around his feet, they nodded in awed agreement. It all added to the apparent mystery as to how the terrible deed was done without a single man springing to alertness.

All the warriors were sure of was that no one man could kill so many without someone hearing something and alerting the others. Or at least no normal man could!

"There are strange forces at work here." came an unidentified whisper. All eyes looked back to where Parrish was now emerging from the water, the women respectfully following several steps behind him. As he headed back towards his own camp they saw the tall man stoop and pick up the severed head by the hair and carry it away with him.

Without another word the watching warriors hurriedly followed Klud as he too set off back towards the Danebury camp. They were glad to get away from the suddenly eerie, silent, almost unearthly camp full of dead men.

Back among the women in their own camp, the warriors watched their Chieftain in silent awe as he stood over his seated wife.

"The man who killed my son." he said flatly, holding the severed head in front of Juli's face. It didn't shock her as much as he had hoped it would. She simply glanced at it briefly, nodded as if she felt the need to give some proof of identification, then looked up into her husband's face. A face that showed no emotion at all.

Juli's face also masked her own painful feelings. She had recently suffered a miss-carriage and lost her baby, gone through the pain of its rejection and felt physically and emotionally exhausted from the ordeal. Yet to her all this was secondary to the grief, anguish and desolation she felt she had inflicted on the man she loved. She accepted that it was her who was solely responsible for the untimely death of Parrish's greatest joy, the son who he had already been so proud of and would now never see. Her husband's face was expressionless but his pain was there for all to see in his actions of the night. As she gazed up at his face she wondered how he could even bear to look at her.

The loss of her baby was very traumatic but the loss of her husband's love was even more so.

There would be no more tears, she decided, the time for that was past. But now her life was empty. All the glories of life that Parrish had shown her were gone. Her love for him was as strong as ever but she was sure it would no longer be returned. It was her duty to do her husband's bidding and to take care of him. This she would still gladly do but it was no longer just a labour of love. Now, for her, there was nothing else left.

As Parrish looked down at his diminutive wife he felt such agonizing pity for her at the loss of her unborn baby. The feelings that welled up inside him when he thought about it choked him so that he could not speak. There were no words of comfort that he could offer Juli. Even if there were, how could she, why should she accept them?

He had let her down when she had needed him most. It was his job and his joy to protect her and look after her and he had failed miserably. That failure had cost him dear. Cost him the life of his son and the love of his wife. He was surprised that she could even look at him. He pitied her too because as a lowly woman in Neolithic Britain, restricted by the tight regime of her society, there was no outlet for her grief and anger.

Of himself, Parrish felt repulsion at the terrible way he had vented his own anger and its appalling costs, not just to the men who were his victims but also to himself. His actions in the night had robbed him of all the things that he valued above all others in this land where he now lived. As well as the almost unbearable loss of his son and his wife's love, he felt that killing the men from Hambledon Hill while they slept had also taken from him the respect of his village's warriors.

Murdering a man while he slept was not honourable and drew no respect. Mass murder in such a dishonourable manner must clearly be unforgivable.

But what hurt Parrish most of all, more than the loss of his men's respect, more than the loss of Juli's love, more even than the loss of his unborn son, the most bitter pill of all to swallow, was his loss of personal honour. His self respect. He had given his word as a respected warrior, a leader of men and as Chieftain of Dane-bre, before all his men and the men of Hambledon Hill. Given his word that he would not attack. Then he had done the very opposite. Gone against his word. Killed them while they slept and had no chance to defend themselves. Murdered them. The act of a liar and a coward and now he was a man without honour.

Parrish looked around at his warriors and their wives who were all watching him in total silence. How they must despise him, he thought. Of course they would not say so because he was their Chieftain, but he knew he no longer had their respect. How could they respect a man with no honour? Parrish could not look them in the eye and lowered his gaze.

"Pack up the camp." he said to no one in particular. "We are returning to Dane-bre. The burial chamber can wait till another day."

The women nodded and silently moved away, glad to start the preparations to break camp and leave this place of death. The warriors still stood watching their Chieftain. There was a long moment of silence before Klud said quietly.

"I will collect up your other trophies my Chieftain."

"NO!" Parrish barked the word, suddenly horrified at the thought of having hanging from the walls of his stall nine skulls of men he had not fought and killed fairly, damning him every time he looked at them. There was one last thing he could do for the men. To restore their stolen honour, even if his own was beyond retrieval.

"They were good men and true to their village. They deserve an honourable passage to the shrine house of the Earth Goddess. Klud, do you think you could find your way to the village of Amaldach-bre?"

The great eyebrows shot up in surprise but he nodded.

"Yes. I am sure it is somewhere in the direction of the setting sun." He pointed away to the west.

At that point another warrior cleared his throat, stepped forward and spoke quietly, still in awe of his tall Chieftain with the suddenly almost supernatural powers.

"I know a man who is of Amaldach-bre." he said. "We meet and trade each year at the gathering point. He has told me that there is a long, high ridge that runs down through the great forest towards the open lowlands. The village is at the end of this ridge."

Combining Klud's vague description with that of the somewhat timid warrior and knowing their present location, Parrish tried to think straight and closed his eyes, picturing a map of central southern England in his head. He decided the ridge they were talking about had to be that of Cranbourne Chase.

A ridge of forested high ground running south-south west from the river Ebble valley to the lowlands of southern Dorset, Cranbourne Chase would in later times be acknowledged as a site of archaeological interest second only to the Salisbury Plain area. Although evidence of Neolithic occupation there is quite scarce, by the end of the Roman era the Chase would bear many marks of pre-historic habitation including dozens of barrows, at least six Iron Age hillforts, several Roman roads and a Bronze Age cursus six miles long. It became a Chase proper early in the seventeenth century when James the first bestowed it on Robert Cecil, then Earl of Salisbury. Even in the twentieth century Cranbourne Chase is still a place of outstanding natural beauty with marvellous views and, for all its occupations by early man and his modern counterpart, still relatively unspoiled.

"Yes." Parrish nodded to himself. I think I know where Amaldach-bre is. Follow this ridge," He pointed up to where the doomed hunting party had first appeared only a day before. "A short way on towards the setting sun. Then this other long, curving ridge will be seen, going away in the opposite direction to Dannu's great temple." He pointed then to the south. "Travel it until it starts to dip down into the open lands below. I think you will find the village there."

Klud just nodded, astounded at the sudden wealth of knowledge Parrish could call upon, knowledge that no other man had. His tall friend never ceased to amaze him. He remembered his conversation with the holy man. Truly, Dannu guided her man in both word and thought.

"I shall deliver their heads to the gates of Amaldach-bre as you ask, my Chieftain." He said eventually, knowing full well that what the Chieftain was asking him to do might very possibly result in his own death at the hands of the understandably angry villagers there. Parrish on the other hand was totally unaware of what Klud had just committed himself to in being prepared if necessary to die on the order of his Chieftain and friend. Fortunately neither man understood the irony in the fact that Parrish imagined his Neolithic friend to think the exact opposite, simply obeying the orders of a man he was duty bound to, the orders of a man he no longer respected because he had no honour.

"No." repeated Parrish. "Their complete bodies must be taken back so they can be offered up to the sky spirits."

"But how?" asked Nam with arms outstretched.

"Stretchers."

Confusion showed on the faces of all the warriors.

"I will show you how to make them." Parrish dropped the severed head unceremoniously onto the ground beside Juli and immediately set to the task, now glad to have something to occupy him.

By midday everything was ready. Stretchers had been made with pairs of cut poles and items of clothing stitched or threaded between them to carry the bodies on. Each of the dead men had been tightly wrapped and now lay upon a stretcher, along with his personal weapons. There were only nine bodies instead of the full ten. Parrish had ordered Tanis' remains to be quartered and the well separated pieces left out for the wild beasts, making it plain that he had no intention of allowing Tanis to sit in the shrine house of Dannu.

The men carried out Parrish's instructions in grim silence. It was a warrior's greatest fear to be denied passage to the shrine house of the Earth Goddess. When a body was taken there by the sky spirits it had to be complete and, if one did not sit with the other waiting warriors, one could not be re-born and walk again in the sun. The soul of a warrior to suffer this fate was lost forever.

All that witnessed the deed knew that the Chieftain was meting out to Tanis the severest punishment of all.

Then it was time to leave.

Two Danebury warriors waited at the ready to carry each stretcher, which left only two 'spare' warriors from the original twenty, along with Parrish, to guide the women safely back to Danebury.

Before the two groups finally went their separate ways, Parrish gave Klud some last minute instructions.

"Take your time and do not exhaust yourselves. When you get to Amaldach-bre tell the people there what has happened if you can but do not take stupid risks. I want all my warriors to return safely to Dane-bre. There has already been enough killing. Even if your honour is insulted." he added, swallowing at that. "Do not challenge them in battle. They are many more, you would surely die and I will not have a war started between two villages just because of my own actions. Do you understand me?"

"I hear your wise words Parrish." Klud offered his friend a small smile. "Do not worry, we will not dishonour you."

To his surprise Parrish actually gave a small laugh, sounding almost like a scoff.

"You are a good friend." He clapped his smaller companion on the shoulder. "Go now and take care, Dannu watches over you."

Klud bowed deeply then went to the warriors under his charge, all standing ready beside their allotted stretchers. They watched as Parrish and his two warriors led the clustered and loaded down women away from the campsite, heading back towards the safety of Danebury hillfort.

"Do you think they will be safe enough with so few warriors as guard?" asked Nam, concerned for the safety of the women but trying to hide it in his voice. After all, his two wives were among them.

"Yes." Klud's reply was emphatic. "Any foolish warriors that would attack Parrish the way his is now would soon find themselves on their way to the shrine house of the Earth Goddess."

Nam was satisfied with the answer. Klud was right. Woe betide any poor souls who attempted to take on their undefeatable Chieftain, who was plainly not in the best of moods.

Klud signalled and his men picked up their burdens and set off in the opposite direction to their women.

Before the two groups eventually lost sight of each other the last pair in the line of stretcher bearers stole a final glance back at the disappearing band of women and its glaringly sparse escort of men, led by their Chieftain. As they usually travelled everywhere so close together, it was suddenly very obvious how distant Parrish stayed from his wife, or was it the other way around?

6

The people of Danebury were at first very concerned and fearful when they saw Parrish's party return depleted of virtually all its men but, after hearing briefly what had happened, their worries turned to complete astonishment!

Once all the families of the missing men had been put at ease and assured that their warriors were still alive, the women immediately began bustling about to bring their homes back to their normal running conditions, making sure that everything would be as it should when the absent men returned. But this apparent, almost over eagerness to work had a second, more immediate purpose. The women's work suddenly necessitated such activities as gathering extra firewood, collecting water and communal baking at the clay ovens, because there they could gather together legitimately in large numbers. Then there was much talk about what had happened and the story of the strange, violent and extraordinary events that had taken place in the little valley below the ridge could be told in its entirety.

Along the same lines but with seemingly more grandeur and right of purpose, the remaining warriors of the village also gathered together to hear the tale from the two men who had accompanied the female group on its return trip. The village grape vine was still as effective as ever and it was not long before all of Danebury knew what had happened and what the tall man had done.

How he had become Dannu's weapon of revenge against the men that had caused the death of his baby, the son of Dannu's man.

How he had risen up in the darkness and moved among the doomed men, protected by his mistress with a cloak of silence and invisibility, and slain them all in her fury!

Whenever Parrish passed by he would receive carefully concealed but never-the-less well meant looks of admiration and awe from the villagers, the events of the last few days another addition to the ever growing stories of impressive, sometimes eerie and mysteriously unexplainable string of events that were slowly making the Chieftain of Dane-bre an almost legendary figure to his people.

Parrish was of course well aware that rumours were circulating around the village but thought them of a different nature to what they actually were. He felt sure they were tales of dishonesty and cold blooded murder.

It had been almost two years now that he had lived among the Neolithic people of southern England but there were still many things that he did not know. He had still not learned that in these early times, where life was hard, tribal unity was everything and death was sometimes only a heartbeat away, murder was a word that had no meaning. You either lived or died. Here it was *how* you lived and *why* you died that was important. The actual means of death was for the most part almost incidental. But Parrish had been born and raised in the twentieth century where death was abhorred and feared, unnecessary death and murder most of all. Life was everything. It had been drummed into him from an early age, from Sunday school bible readings and children's fables, right through his education years and on into the Army. Indeed, part of his reason for joining up was to enable him to protect his family, friends, his country and its way of life. Mercilessly murdering nine innocent men, he didn't count Tanis as innocent, struck at the very core of his being and sense of righteousness, what the people in these early times call their honour. The terrible deed had robbed him of his self esteem, that vital belief in oneself, and Parrish could not come to terms with his conscience.

Although the people of Danebury still greatly admired and honoured their Chieftain, Parrish could not see it. He was lost to his tortured soul and his modern day reasoning which he had still to learn had little meaning here. And yet he was still immensely grateful to the people under his charge for it was only the responsibility of their wellbeing that kept him from totally submerging into a pit of self pity and personal loathing from which he might never emerge. There were still things that needed to be done and a village of people, dependent upon him, that needed to be taken care of. It was his lifeline.

The villagers knew that something was terribly wrong with their Chieftain but did not know what. His thinking was beyond their comprehension and all they could do was watch in sorrow as Parrish passed among them. Doing the right thing for his village, as always, but it was plain to see that now his heart was not in it. He had for some sad reason lost his enthusiasm, his love of life. Not only for the village but also for his friends and, most painful of all for the downtrodden women of Danebury, his wife.

Juli continued to look after her husband, prepare food, warm their house and do the hundred and one other daily chores that made up the day to day running of a warrior's home life. But the strange closeness between them, usually so plain to see even though they tried to disguise it, was now glaring in its absence. Now they barely spoke to each other, and yet there was so much to say. Juli was so terribly saddened by the loss of her baby but could not find the comfort she so badly needed in the arms of her husband. Whenever the women gathered and tried to talk of the sadness in the house of Parrish, Juli would cry openly. The other women felt for the poor girl but for her theirs was cold comfort.

Parrish too suffered in silence, spending many hours atop his grassy knoll overlooking the village and watching as the little community went about its business. The people had long since gotten used to his constant scrutiny but knew their Chieftain was now using his high vantage point as a place of solitude. His constantly dour mood and inner sadness seemed never ending and somehow crept into every corner of the camp, settling like an invisible, smothering blanket over everything and the village of Dane-bre became a sadder, colder place which even the early summer sun struggled in vain to warm.

Tomps had walked up the grassy slope watching, as always, with intense curiosity the tall man who sat motionless at the top, and was about to speak to his Chieftain when Parrish suddenly held up his hand, demanding silence. The young warriors words hung unsaid on his tongue, mouth poised in slack silence. His words were important enough, concerning the preparations for the next hunting trip which was only a short time away, but they were instantly forgotten when Tomps saw the sudden alertness on his Chieftains face.

Parrish rose smartly to his feet and the lad looked briefly up in admiration at the man who towered over him, before turning and following the Chieftains line of sight.

Approaching slowly from the south west, still quite a long way off, was what looked like a hunting party. A big one. Without a word Parrish began to head off down towards the village where another warrior had already appeared at the run, clearly on his way to tell Parrish what he now already knew.

Tomps made his own assessment of the situation and pointed back towards Parrish's cabin.

"Shall I get your bow?" he called out after his Chieftain.

"No need." Parrish didn't even bother to look back at the lad, continuing to stare away at the distant cluster of men even as he walked. "I think they are ours."

Even at the extreme distance and without the benefit of binoculars, the approaching group looked about the right size, although he couldn't be sure. If it were the Danebury warriors Parrish mused, then they had made quite reasonable time considering the rather ambling pace that the people around here travelled at, for they had been gone barely five days. So then, a day or so from the little valley of death to the hillfort of Amaldach-bre and three more for the total return trip. Parrish made a mental note of the extra information.

At first Tomps didn't understand the odd sounding phrase but quickly fell in beside the tall man and together they walked on down into the village and met the approaching warrior.

"A large party comes." The man pointed away in the direction of the distant troupe.

"Yes." Parrish nodded. "Perhaps they are the rest of my warriors returning from Amaldach-bre," he paused, "but we should be ready if they are not."

"It is already done, my Chieftain."

"Good."

Parrish dismissed him with the briefest of bows and the warrior nodded in acknowledgment, before dashing off back the way he had come, to collect his weapons and join the others up on the parapet of the defence wall.

Almost casually, or so it appeared to those who did not know the

Chieftain well, Parrish sauntered up and joined his warriors upon the parapet. They were tense as they waited for the men to draw nearer but Parrish was pretty certain that he had been right in his first assessment of the approaching party. Everyone stood in silence as the troupe of men approached.

Sure enough, it was indeed the rest of the Danebury burial chamber party and there was an almost tangible sense of relief from the men lined up along the wall. They all knew how depleted a force they would have presented to a large attacking group if it had been necessary to fight a battle.

Everyone made their way from the wall to the entrance of the hillfort. There was muted but excited babbling and speculation from among the men, curious to know what had happened to their compatriots on their unprecedented mission. The warriors at the gate were soon joined by most of the women of the village, who just seemed to sidle quietly up in ones and twos and join on to the rear of the crowd. Parrish was the only man who seemed to notice this, understanding that most of the womenfolk were more attached to their men than they would care to admit.

At first Parrish watched impassively as the returning men trooped in, glad that they were at last safe, and warm in the knowledge that he had done the right thing in returning the bodies. This mood quickly changed as he counted them past and realized that there were only seventeen men present instead of eighteen!

The last man in the gate was Narn and a sudden feeling of dread clutched at Parrish's heart. Grabbing the Neolithic warrior roughly by the arm he dragged him unceremoniously off to the side and asked urgently.

"Where is Klud?" It was difficult to hide the concern in his voice and even harder to disguise his sinking feeling of trepidation. Had he sent his good friend to his death?

Narn was unprepared for the sudden, hard questioning and the hot intensity in his Chieftains eyes made him want to take a step back. He found he could not break the grip on his arm, Parrish's hand clamping down on his bicep hard enough to make him wince.

"He .... he is still at Amaldach-bre."

"But still alive?"

Narn nodded vigorously.

Parrish turned from Narn and addressed the massed people before him.

"All but one have now returned. Well done my warriors, I know you did not understand my reasons for returning the men from Amaldach-bre but you carried out the task with honour. Return to your families now and rest. I thank you all." He bowed his head to the men.

There were murmurs. It was great praise from a great man and all the men were honoured to have their deeds publicly acknowledged. Everyone bowed deeply back to their Chieftain. The murmurs died away to silence and there was a long pause before Tomps finally voiced the question that everyone was thinking.

"What will happen to Klud, my Chieftain?"

At least the young warrior had put it so that it was not a direct question, asking the Chieftain to explain what his next actions might be, and so did not insult him. The boy was learning the art of being a good warrior, knowing when to fight and how if possible to be able to prevent one if the odds were not good. A sort of basic, Stone Age diplomacy.

Parrish smiled at the lad, a rare expression from him in the last few days. When he spoke his voice was filled with a certainty that was designed to assure those who now waited for his answer.

"I will attend to that." He said slowly and with much deliberation. Then he clapped his hands together and waved away the people. "Go now, away to your homes and families. Rest and eat. When the holy man returns, we must have a ceremony of thanks for your safe return." That brought smiles to the small sea of faces. Immediately, they started to disperse, the women smoothly falling in a pace or two behind their men. As Tomps turned to leave Parrish stepped close to him and said quietly.

"Do not be concerned. Klud will be at the celebration also, if I have anything to do with it. I feel Dannu is watching over him."

Tomps looked up at his Chieftain. He knew the tall man spoke true and was a great warrior. The young man's faith in Parrish was unshakable and the calm words were enough. He smiled gratefully, puffed out his chest and set off towards his family hut, his tiny wife Karin close behind.

There was no doubt either how she felt about the leader of her village. He frightened her. He seemed so powerful that she was suddenly very glad he was for the village of Dane-bre, and not against it. In a strange way she felt almost sorry for the people of Amaldach-bre. They could not know they were in great danger, but the weapon of the wrath of Dannu was looking in their direction.

Parrish simply watched the pair go then turned back to Narn who still waited patiently beside him.

"Come to my hut and tell me exactly what happened. Leave nothing out."

Narn simply bowed, a Chieftains request was a warrior's order. The pair headed in silence towards the centre of the village and the thatched hut with the ornately carved entrance porch that was the official residence of the head of Dane-bre.

The two men sat on the woven mats that covered the floor of the circular hut. They were the only items in it and Narn found the emptiness rather eerie and slightly intimidating. Parrish allowed the warrior a few moments to gather his thoughts before speaking.

"Tell me what happened at Amaldach-bre." He said quietly.

"We set off and followed your directions." Narn's voice was steady and even. "It took a day's travel to reach the village. It is high on a hill at the end of the great ridge and can be clearly seen from a long way away. When we tried to approach, the warriors there shot arrows at us but we knew it was only a warning. If they had waited till we drew closer they could easily have killed us."

Parrish listened in total silence, face expressionless. He knew the people who witnessed the strange entourage approach their village would have been burning with curiosity. He knew he would if the situation were reversed. If he hadn't been so sure of that fact, to send his warriors to Amaldach-bre would have been gambling unnecessarily with their lives.

Narn half expected a question at this point and waited a few moments before realizing that none would be forthcoming. He continued.

"We did not know what to do. Then Klud decided to do as you had done. He laid down his weapons and walked slowly up to the main gate, asking to speak to the Chieftain there. We were all sure that he would be quickly killed."

"The bloody fool." said Parrish quietly in English but smiled anyway. Klud had balls all right and Parrish was suddenly filled with fresh admiration for his absent friend. Narn's eyebrows went up in silent question at the strange, unintelligible words that the Chieftain was known to mumble when he thought deep thoughts. Parrish waved away the silent query.

"Go on."

"The warriors of Amaldach-bre did not kill him. Several armed men slipped out of the gate and took him inside." It was plain by the look on the smaller man's face that even now, as he relayed the story to his Chieftain, the strange events of the last few days still amazed him. "No one knows what Klud said to those inside but after a while the gate swung wide and we were told to leave our weapons behind and bring in the dead men. I shouted back that we would not do so because we would all be killed." Narn made a point of telling Parrish this, proud of the fact that without guidance he had made what was in effect a command decision.

"Then their Chieftain appeared and gave his word of honour that this would not happen. We carried the men in." Parrish nodded. It still impressed him, even after the length of time he had spent with these people, how much faith they put on a man's word.

"And Klud?" he asked eagerly. "What of Klud?"

"All the warriors of Amaldach-bre were gathered, waiting for us inside their fort. They were many, we were few. They had weapons and we did not." There was a sharp intake of breath and Narn leaned towards Parrish, lowering his voice even though there was no one else present. "I must admit to you Parrish that I thought the Earth Goddess was getting ready to gather us all up then."

It was the closest any warrior would ever get to admitting fear and Parrish gave a knowing smile.

"You acted with great bravery and honour. Dane-bre is proud to count you as one of its men. But what of Klud?"

"He was being held alongside their Chieftain, a dagger at his throat. Their leader told us to lay the bodies down. Then he said that we were free to go and to tell you that he wanted to speak to the man who had killed his warriors. To be sure that you would come he had decided to keep Klud. He said that if you did not come he would kill him without honour and not allow the sky spirits to take him to the great shrine house of Dannu."

Parrish could well imagine the dread that Klud would have felt at such a threat. His friend's faith in his religion was absolute.

Narn laid a concerned hand on his Chieftains arm.

"Klud is my friend too, but you are Chieftain of Dane-bre. He knows this. You should not go Parrish. They want to take your head."

"I know." Parrish rose slowly to his feet. "But he is my friend also and he was doing my bidding. I cannot leave him there. And there is another thing."

"What is that?" Narn stood too and followed his Chieftain outside, squinting for a moment against the summer sunshine.

"They do not know who they make threats at!"

Sucking in a great breath of the sweet air, tinged with the aroma of cooking food and the tang of wood smoke, Parrish suddenly felt the life begin to flow through him again. He had just been given a task to do. Even better, a dangerous one too! He wasn't fully sure why but he felt as if he had just received a reviving shot in the arm. Here perhaps was a chance to put right a small part of the great wrong he had done. It wasn't much in the way of personal redemption but at least it was a start. The adrenalin began to flow, somehow accentuated by the recklessness that comes with the lack of worry about personal safety that befalls someone who has lost his self-respect. He turned and looked down at Nam, a cold glint in his eye.

"I must go, and go alone. I thank you for your words and honour you for your bravery." He bowed to the warrior. "But now I must go and make ready and be gone before nightfall."

Narn bowed deeply back in response to his Chieftains gesture but Parrish was already striding purposefully up towards his cabin even before the action was completed. He stared after the tall man for a long moment before dashing excitedly off to tell the other warriors the latest development in this extraordinary saga.

7

Juli watched in silence while Parrish readied himself for his trip. He had made all the preparations himself, not once asking for or expecting any assistance from his wife, and she had not dared to offer it.

He carried just a single litre of water, in the plastic water bottle that was an integral part of his webbing, and only enough dried meat to fill one kidney pouch and the left side front ammo pouch. The other compartments of his webbing carried all the other personal military kit that had come back with him from the distant future. Across his back was the leather quiver that carried his long arrows. It had been made by the only other important Neolithic woman in Parrish's life, but she had sadly died the winter before. He wore his combat jacket and in one hand held his great bow. The long woollen cape that usually lay across his broad shoulders and hung down to his calves was now limp on a peg beside the doorway and Juli was painfully aware of it. Parrish had rejected it in favour of the camouflage and ease of movement offered by his jacket. Yet to Juli, as he stood before her wearing all his personal items and leaving behind all the goods he had accumulated since arriving at Dane-bre, it looked as if he were leaving permanently. She somehow felt she had been instrumental in driving him away.

Parrish nodded to himself in personal satisfaction. From his combat boots and dark tanned buckskin trousers right through to his jacket and the webbing that snuggled reassuringly around his midriff, he felt ready for action. As if about to embark on a military exercise. The bow and arrows weren't quite standard Army issue but he knew he was at least as well armed as his potential opponents.

After completing his final check he made to leave, pausing for a moment in the doorway. Turning to face his wife, their eyes met. He desperately wanted to go to her, hold her, tell her goodbye and not to worry. But he doubted that after the way he had failed her she would even be able to bear his touch.

Juli in turn wanted to run to her husband, hold him tight and feel his strong arms about her, but did not, for she knew he despised her for killing his son.

And so he just stared across the room at her in total silence, no discernible expression on his face although the eyes still showed his pain. Juli respectfully lowered her eyes. When she looked up again the doorway was empty.

Parrish made his way across the village towards Klud's hut and, once there, called out for the warriors first wife. She appeared almost immediately and bowed respectfully, keeping her eyes down. Even so, it was impossible not to notice the clothing and equipment he wore and the determination in his voice when he finally spoke.

"I am going for Klud." Short and to the point.

The Neolithic woman did not doubt for a moment that Parrish would accomplish such a task, although just how and what would be necessary for him to do to manage such a gargantuan feat she could not even guess at. She only knew that such a task would be fraught with danger. Parrish just received a silent nod in reply.

"If Klud has any spare weapons I would like to have them. I think he may have need of them. A bow perhaps?"

There was indeed a bow and the woman fetched it, re-appearing from her hut with it, plus a quiver full of the absent man's short, Neolithic arrows. In her other hand she carried a war club with a polished stone head. Parrish had never seen one before and assumed that it was normally used only for ceremonial purposes. His friend’s wife stepped up close to him and held the weapons out. Parrish slung the quiver and bow across his back beside his own and, after briefly inspecting the polished club, tucked it into his webbing belt on the opposite side to his knife. The small woman then stepped even closer and said quietly, without looking into Parrish’s eyes.

"Take care, my Chieftain. Come home safely." Parrish was

touched by her concern for him.

"It will be so." He replied softly. "I fear nothing now. Klud will soon be back with his family, and I feel that Dannu is with me." he added not completely truthfully, hoping to quell any fears the woman might have.

She looked up at him then, hoping to see Parrish smiling as he so often used to. His face was grim. The confusion on her face was plain to see and Parrish reached out and tenderly touched her cheek. If he could not talk to his own wife, he knew he could talk to this caring woman and it was somewhat of a relief to voice his worries to someone.

"Mother, I do not fear for myself anymore but for all the others."

"Others?" Yes, it was a question from a woman but they were alone and Klud's wife felt somehow compelled to ask it. She suddenly needed to know the answer as much as she knew the tall man needed to answer it.

Parrish put it in its simplest term. Terms that anyone in these Neolithic times would instantly understand.

"There will be trophies, Mother. I feel it. Many trophies."

She gasped at the enormity of his last words. If the words had come from anyone else but Dannu's man she might have thought them an idle boast or just wishful thinking. But from the tall man who stood before her they were words of undeniable certainty. An announcement of bad things to come. A prophecy of death. She wished she could close her ears to the sounds.

If Parrish recognized and understood what she felt, he certainly didn't show it. All he did was offer her the briefest of nods, then strode away.

When he reached the main gate all the warriors of the village were there. Several immediately volunteered to go with him, Tomps among them. The Chieftain waved his men silent.

"I am grateful for your offers but I must go alone. It is me they want and also, I intend to travel fast." He turned to Gant, clapping him on the shoulder. "I must leave you in charge again my friend."

"It is my honour Parrish." The warrior bowed deeply. Tomps stepped up beside Gant and Parrish eyed him sternly for a moment. The lad was once again hoping to claim his position as the temporary Chieftain's right hand man.

Parrish did not object but wanted him to understand that it was not a position to be taken lightly.

"Watch this man and learn." He said to the boy, patting Gant on the shoulder. "He is wise, patient and fair, yet also strong and brave. A great warrior. One day you may be warrior enough to take charge of a whole village."

Tomps bowed deeply to his Chieftain and Gant's chest puffed out with pride at such an accolade. Parrish then fixed the older warrior with the same stern stare.

"I leave my village in your hands." He said gravely, not needing to over emphasize the gravity of the responsibility for he was sure it was well understood, then turned without another word and went out through the gate. Everyone watched in silence.

When he reached the bottom of the path, beyond the ends of the defence ditch, he broke into an easy dog trot and moved swiftly and steadily off towards the west and the setting sun.

With the eyes of the entire village on the tall, camouflage clad man carrying two bows across his back, no one noticed the diminutive figure of Juli standing on the threshold of the Chieftains cabin, also looking out over the Neolithic landscape and watching her husband heading towards what everyone knew was almost certain death. She watched until he had disappeared into the distant tree line and the vastness of the great forest, then went back into the cabin, slumped down onto the dry earth floor, held her face in her hands, and sobbed.

Parrish made good time, continuing to jog along, threading his way deftly between the thick trunks, until the light finally went. Then he slowed his pace to a steady walk and pushed on through the night, listening with interest to the varied and sometimes mysteriously unidentifiable sounds of the land and the different life it seemed to live when under a blanket of darkness. Unable now to travel with any real speed he made use of the time to consider a plan of attack for when he finally reached Hambledon Hill. Of course, not knowing what he would find when he got there left the whole affair very open ended. Too open ended, but that was unavoidable.

One thing he did know was that surprise and stealth was clearly the order of the day for this mission. What else could one man hope to use to his advantage against an entire village? He was relying heavily on the people of Hambledon Hill knowing full well that it was at least three days journey between their village and Danebury and that they would not expect his arrival for at least six days, even assuming that he accepted their terms and set off immediately. Parrish allowed a smile to cross his determined features. He fully intended to be in sight of Hambledon Hill by nightfall tomorrow. Travelling thirty or so miles cross country in twenty four hours was easily within the reach of a fit, trained soldier. If he made really good time he would even have plenty of time to assess the defences of the hillfort before he moved in. And that was the hard part. Somehow he had to figure a way into the fort, working of course under the cover of darkness, release Klud and get out again, all without raising the alarm.

To find his friend, somewhere within the confines of the unfamiliar village, he would first have to identify the hut in which he was being held. If Parrish were Chieftain there, he would almost certainly have ordered Klud tied up and a guard stationed at the entrance to the prisoner's hut. He hoped his assessment was right. Spotting the guard would make finding Klud a lot easier and save risky time and effort.

Parish ran several different scenarios through his mind but they all ended up being simply variations on his original plan. The most pressing problem would be gaining access to the hillfort. Danebury's defences were most efficient and he expected no less from those of Hambledon Hill. Whatever he came up against when he got there would simply have to be dealt with somehow. It was certainly something to ponder on as he passed steadily on through the dark night. With no real answer coming to mind, he finally stopped in an isolated clump of tall trees and settled down for a couple of hours sleep. He would be on his way once more at first light.

With the arrival of the morning sun, the countryside seemed clean and fresh. Summer was upon it and the forests were a glorious emerald green. Where the woodland thinned out towards the more open land the hillsides became dotted with individual trees, mostly great oaks or beeches, that splashed the rolling pasture with dark puddles of cool shade.

Although Parrish was moving with keen intent across the chalk uplands of central southern England, he could still take time to appreciate its beauty. Small white clouds floated across the bright blue sky above him and the soft shadows they cast upon the landscape caused constantly changing hues of light and dark. The whole land seemed alive, and Parrish with it. The sweet scented air surged into his body with every deep breath that he took.

He no longer trotted, settling into the rhythmic pace of alternately walking then double marching, the tried and tested military method of moving quickly from one position to another. The Royal Marine Commandos called it 'tabbing', tab standing for Tactical Approach to Battle. Parrish knew he could keep the strenuous pace up for hours and in his super fit state it now seemed more easy to do than he could ever remember. It was as if he were somehow slicing through the Neolithic landscape like a knife, it appearing almost to part before him and aid him on his journey. Occasionally he would spot some form of wildlife, usually a deer or two, and they simply watched him pass by, totally unafraid. And he knew why. He was a lone wolf, stalking through the Stone Age countryside with a specific victim in mind, and the other creatures that shared the land with him somehow knew it and allowed him to pass close by without feeling threatened. It unexplainably gave Parrish a feeling of great power and he spared himself a few moments to revel in it. Only when he finally found himself wondering if Dannu really was with him and assisting him along his way across her land, parting it for him to allow easy passage, did he finally reign in his wild imaginings, admonish himself for allowing his silly flight of fancy, and once again applied himself to the daunting task ahead.

And yet things did seem to continue to go so smoothly. The river crossings were accomplished with consummate ease and as he travelled up and along the ridges of the southern uplands it seemed he did not, could not put a foot wrong. The land seemed almost to fly beneath his feet and the kilometres quickly began to string out behind him. For a short, glorious time, Parrish was at one with nature, alone in the vastness of the wild. Just one more creature among all the creatures under the protective umbrella and ever watchful eye of the Earth Goddess. The tall stranger felt strange no more and was it seemed a small but integral piece of some great mysterious scheme. The freedom of the world was his and with the earth power flowing through him his skin tingled, nerve endings buzzed and he felt, despite the deadly danger he travelled towards, strangely euphoric. As if he were capable of almost anything.

8

The sun was going down, its redness seeming to bleed into the Neolithic landscape. Parrish sat motionless beside the trunk of a huge, sprawling oak tree, careful to position himself below the skyline of the end of the ridge that was Cranbourne Chase, so not to present a visible silhouette on the horizon. Across the valley from his position, on an isolated hill with an elongated brow, its low profile stark against the setting sun, was Amaldach-bre hillfort.

Parrish had arrived, just as expected, shortly before nightfall and was making good use of the last of the daylight to get his bearings and make a preliminary assessment of the camps defences before the light finally went.

Unlike the circular layout of his home fort, Amaldach-bre was shaped like a giant teardrop. The more rounded end was sited at the southern limit of the brow, the pointed end stretching northwards towards the centre of the ridge and encompassing within its point a small, slightly higher area that had raised trestles on it, standing proud of the ground. Parrish instantly recognized these rough constructions and knew that was the place where the dead of the village were offered up to the sky spirits. Excarnation of bodies, the cadavers held up for the attention of carrion birds. Similar he knew, to the ways of the North American Indians. He was still too far away to see but knew also that nine of those trestles would be occupied.

Parrish turned his nose up. A bit too close to the village itself for his liking. If the wind was in the wrong direction things would smell just a bit ripe in a week or so, but he could clearly see that the village was a bit pushed for space along the hilltop. Just beyond the walled area of the camp at its excarnation end, at the highest point of the hill and somewhat impressive as the sun set behind it, was a long burial mound with a single standing stone at its entrance. Where the bones of the dead lay.

Watching in silence as the shadows drew ever longer until they finally faded and merged with the growing darkness, Parrish set his mind to the task of entering the fort. Tactically it was sound to attempt the wall where it was furthest from any of the occupying personnel. That meant a stealthy approach from the direction of the long barrow and scaling the wall near the trestles. Unknown at that time to the twentieth century man, his choice was doubly wise.

To the people of these Neolithic times it was considered most disrespectful to pass through the area set aside for offering up to Dannu the bodies of her people. It was sacred ground and not to be defiled by merely passing. It was a place never walked upon except for the delivering of the dead, and then only in the guiding accompaniment of a holy one. The people knew that no one who had respect for and fear of the Earth Goddess would dare to insult her by trespassing there.

Because everyone knew this and would not even consider defiling the domain of the dead and risk their own lives by insulting Dannu, the area around it was not as heavily defended as the rest of the village, the wall being lower and the defence ditch shallower. Even so, there was still another palisade wall that separated the village from its burial area and that wall alone was a good three meters high.

Thus it was not considered by the occupants of Hambledon Hill to be any more lacking in defence than the other parts of the fort with its sheer, timber lined walls and deeply cut ditches, because no self respecting warrior born under Dannu's watchful eye would even consider attacking from over the burial ground. Parrish however, was not born of these times, considered himself a man of no self respect and did not fear the Earth Goddess in the least.

He had watched for movement and as far as he could tell there were no guards along the walls. Clearly he was not expected for at least another few days, something that he had been greatly relying on.

As the night drew on a partial moon began to show and light clouds that floated occasionally by shrouded its dull incandescence, intermittently blotting out the landscape with a blanket of darkness. Parrish settled down to wait, giving the people of the hillfort ample time to get comfortable in their beds. He chewed slowly on a few pieces of jerky but stopped when he thought about the meat and how Juli must have carefully dried it. Thinking about her interrupted his concentration. Besides, it hurt too much.

He watched the moon climb slowly into the sky and the campfires that glowed against the darkness dim one by one, until he was certain that all inside Amaldach-bre were asleep. Then he waited some more, listening with a detached interest to the night sounds of the land as they carried across it in the still air.

It was time.

Parrish had no way to tell but was sure that it was well after midnight. In a few more hours the sun would be coming up once more. He blacked out his white and highly visible face by applying a liberal helping of his issue camouflage cream, smearing it across his face and the backs of his hands in jagged lines, to break up the regularity of his features.

From now on everything was tactical. He crept silently down through the trees to the valley floor. Crouching beside the last big tree before the open ground he looked up at the bare hillside that rose ahead of him, taking in its contours. It was almost completely lacking in cover apart from a spattering of low hawthorn bushes along its steep flanks. They would have to do.

He took off the two bows and quivers and propped them up against the tree's broad trunk. There would be no use for them inside the camp, he reasoned. If he were discovered while inside Amaldach-bre there would be no chance of him shooting his way out against the forces of an entire village.

Besides, the long weapons would be a hindrance while scaling the ditches and walls. Even so, he really didn't like leaving his unique bow behind in the dark but, as good as he was with it, even he couldn't shoot things he couldn't see!

Making a mental note of the tree and its location, he set off up the steep slope, keeping as best he could to the sparse shadows of the bushes and pacing himself to stay fresh. It took a good half hour to reach the summit unobserved, deliberately cresting the brow on the far side of the burial mound and being sure to keep it between himself and the camp. He allowed himself the luxury of a few minutes to catch his breath before starting his silent assault.

Moving swiftly now on the balls of his feet, he worked his way alongside the long barrow, pausing for a moment behind the single standing stone before breaking cover to dart to the edge of the ditch, slide down into it and scrabble quickly up the other side to reach the base of the palisade wall. Parrish crouched there in its dark shadow. To his surprise he found himself not in the least bit afraid, rather in fact relishing the adrenalin buzz as hot blood thundered round his body, heightening the feelings of nerve tingling tension and that familiar gripping tightness in his gut. All his senses seemed suddenly acute and he was very aware of his ears, eyes and that unexplainable sixth sense, all reaching out into the darkness that surrounded him.

The wall rose up above his crouched form. Standing tall and raising an arm to roughly gauge its height, he guessed it at no more than three or four meters. He allowed himself a brief smile. The brick wall on the assault course at the Light Infantry barracks outside Winchester was taller and he knew he could scale that with ease. Stepping back a few paces to give himself a short run up, he dashed forward and leapt for the top, finding a good purchase with his hands around the neck of one of the timber uprights. Swinging his leg up onto the uneven parapet gained him his third anchor point and, with a heave of his body he was over, landing skilfully on his feet with a quiet thud inside the compound.

Immediately ahead were the trestles, long legged tables rising into the night. Between their crooked legs it was possible to see the second wall that was the boundary of the village itself. The moonlight illuminated another three meter wall although this time it was not pre-empted by a ditch.

Deliberately not pausing among the trestles and the grim contents they held, Parrish had no wish to be further reminded of the men he had murdered, he moved in silence through the wooden constructions and on across the tract of open ground, painfully aware of his blatant, bare exposure to anyone who might choose to look in his direction. The moon felt like it was a spotlight, shining solely on him.

Falling gratefully into the shadow at the base of the second wall, there were a few heart stopping moments as he waited, listening to see if a sudden shout would go up, the alarm be raised and all his plans come to nothing. His straining ears heard no sound. With a vault he quickly scaled the second wall and rolled over the top, landing in a well balanced crouch atop the earthen walkway behind it. Now he could see the village of Amaldach-bre laid out before him as he looked southward towards the entrance gate across the thatched roofs of the huts.

Two things were immediately obvious. The first was that he was in effect looking at the back of the village and its buildings. He knew that if there were any tell tale guards they would almost certainly be posted at the entrance to the prisoner's hut. From his current position he could see neither entrances nor any visible guards. The second was that the moon was shining directly into his face and *he* was eminently visible!

Keeping to his low crouch, Parrish scampered in a clockwise direction along the parapet of the wall, moving as quickly as he could around the perimeter of the camp till he had gained the shadow of the south eastern quarter of the barrier. As he became enveloped once more in the comforting darkness, the entrances of the huts started to become visible. Still he could see no guards. He mentally cursed.

Sidling along a bit further towards the huge main gate, the entrance to the great central shrine hut at last became visible. It had previously been blocked from his view by one of the thatched conical huts in front of it. There, shuffling his feet with tired boredom, his spear propped up against the wall behind him, was a lone sentry.

Gotcha, thought Parrish almost gleefully. Only one man and he looks half asleep. It was almost as good as he could have hoped for. He slid noiselessly down the earthen bank of the walkway and disappeared into the black shadow cast by the hut nearest to him. Always keeping buildings between himself and his intended victim, Parrish moved stealthily closer, circling around to approach from the rear of the great shrine hut. Flattening up against the rough, mud daubed wall the tall man scanned the still deathly quiet village briefly, then sidled silently along it, edging ever closer to the unsuspecting sentry. The Neolithic man eventually came into view, still at his post, while Parrish was still six or seven meters away, as close as he could get without being seen. It was all down to surprise now.

With a muted grunt of effort Parrish burst into the sentry's view, running at full speed towards the man, and reached him just as the half asleep guard was turning to see what the noise was. Before he had a chance to shout any warning Parrish leapt, hurling himself bodily at the smaller man. His full weight took the guard squarely across the chest and they both crashed to the hard packed earth, the little warrior with the wind driven from his lungs while Parrish changed his fall into a clumsy forward roll and leapt swiftly to his feet.

The stricken Amaldach-bre man gasped for breath, only managing to get up onto all fours before Parrish closed with him and delivered a vicious, bone jarring, full powered kick to the head. The tremendous effort of the kick almost snapped the unfortunate warrior upright and he flipped over onto his back and thudded limply to the ground. Parrish unceremoniously grasped the man's buckskin tunic by the shoulders and dragged him quickly out of sight through the door blanket of the shrine hut and into the walled corridor behind it. Once there, a brief check of the limp figure revealed that he was dead, his neck broken.

Head bowed, Klud sat on the straw in the mouth of one of the stalls of the hut, its position approximately halfway around the building between the entrance and the huge statue of the Earth Goddess opposite. He sat with his back to one of the upright pillars that supported the roof. His hands were securely lashed together behind it. The hut was dully illuminated by several tallow lamps. Klud was not at his best, struggling with the severe stomach cramps that assaulted his compact frame periodically, and so paid no attention to the occasional sounds or mutters of the Amaldach-bre holy man who bustled about behind the statue. Only the holy man's shadow was visible, projected against the back wall of the hut by the lamps that were illuminating his living quarters. It flicked back and forth along the wall although the man himself was not visible. Whatever he was doing in his living space this late at night held no interest for the Danebury man and he did not even bother to look up whenever the muttering grew loud.

A sudden, light touch on his shoulder did however make him raise his head. His eyes widened with surprise as recognition dawned and he opened his mouth to speak. Parrish clapped a hand over his friend's mouth and signalled him to remain silent. Klud nodded and the firm hand was removed. With a reassuring wink, the tall man moved silently across to the base of the statue of Dannu.

Klud craned his neck to watch in horrified fascination as his

Chieftain rose to full height, the dull light casting his somehow eerie, undulating dark shadow across the statue. The tall man paused for a moment, to his observer never had he looked more full of deadly menace, then quietly but deliberately cleared his throat. The sound seeming briefly to fill the hollowness of the hut.

The sounds of bustle from beyond the statue stopped abruptly, there was a long moment of silence then the holy man appeared, curiosity about the strange sound clear to see on his features. He took a few steps out onto the floor looking towards the lone prisoner, evidently expecting him to be the source of the sound.

Klud's return gaze was directed not at the little shaman but behind him and the flower and feather man naturally turned to follow the warrior's line of sight. The look of amazement on his face was almost comical as he turned and suddenly found the towering form of Parrish standing directly behind him. For a brief moment there was complete silence as he looked up into the darkly painted face with the cold eyes that stared straight back. He finally opened his mouth to speak. 'Dannu's man!' were the words he was about to gasp, but never got the chance. Parrish thought he was about to raise the alarm and quickly silenced the Neolithic shaman with a single, straight armed and blurringly fast punch to the chin, the smacking impact sounding extra loud against the blanket of silence around them. The little man sprawled backwards on the ground, raising dust.

Parrish knelt to check that he was simply unconscious then grabbed the prostrate man by the collar, dragged him across to where Klud still sat, and slung him roughly into the stall. He landed limply with no more than a soft rustle on the deep straw. And all the time the Danebury warrior watched in amazed silence.

Parrish drew his knife and cut his friends bonds. Klud rubbed at his sore wrists and eyed the unmoving holy man with trepidation.

"Do not worry." Parrish whispered. "He is not dead, just sleeping. He will awake later with only a sore chin. I have no wish to kill a holy one."

"How did you get here?" Klud nodded in satisfaction at the assurance of the shaman's safety but could not conceive how any one man could get past the defences of an entire village. The barriers here were not much different to those of Dane-bre, he knew. Were they really so ineffective against one determined man? He knew too that it should have been impossible for his tall friend even to be here in Amaldach-bre so soon. Had not the message for him to come only been sent a few days earlier?

"With the help of Dannu." Parrish winked again. If it was meant to be a joke it was totally lost on Klud. He nodded solemnly.

"Here." Parrish handed him his polished stone axe. The Neolithic man grinned with recognition and hefted it in his hand, feeling the familiarity of the weapon. "Only use it if it is absolutely necessary my friend. We must rely on silence and stealth to leave this place or we will never leave it alive. Do you understand?"

Klud nodded and Parrish led off back to the entrance of the great hut. The Neolithic warrior shot a quick glance up at the huge effigy of Dannu. She seemed to be simply observing the actions of her man with a detached interest, the smooth curves of the stonework aglow with the light from the lamps.

It was all beyond Klud's comprehension. He was just a simple man doing his best to live a good life in a suddenly more complicated land. He hoped his Chieftain understood more of what was going on than he did. Fighting off another sharp attack of the cramps he ran across to join his tall saviour at the mouth of the corridor and together they made their way along it to the entrance.

Parrish stepped totally unconcerned over the still warm body of the sentry. Klud cast his battle hardened warriors eye over the corpse. Although definitely dead, the Neolithic man could not pinpoint the actual cause of death. There appeared to be no marks on the body. For a brief moment he stared at Parrish's broad back and wandered just what his tall, mysterious friend, Chieftain of his village and Dannu's man, was really capable of.

9

Once outside the shrine hut, the pair made their way in silence to the hillfort entrance, darting from shadow to shadow, zigzagging across the village. Klud knew that Dannu was with them for nothing stirred, the entire place seemed to be unnaturally quiet, although perhaps Klud's opinion was such because he had hardly ever been awake at this hour and had no real idea quite how still the hours just before the dawn were.

Either way, they reached the huge gate without incident. Parrish pushed back the long wooden locking bar, wincing with every creak and groan as the timber slid dryly through its guide brackets. Klud kept watch, axe always at the ready. At last the bar was clear and both men eagerly tugged back the heavy gate until there was a big enough gap for them to slip through. They were out.

Parrish immediately broke into a jog and sped down the long, sloping road that lead away from Amaldach-bre, Klud only one step behind him. The tall man was in the process of mentally patting himself on the back in congratulation of his successful jail break when he heard his friend stifle a groan and crash to the hard packed earth of the pathway. He turned to find Klud curled up on the ground, clutching at his midriff and grimacing in pain. Dashing back he quickly knelt beside the fallen warrior.

"What is wrong?" he whispered, the concern clear in his voice.

"I am sorry my Chieftain." Klud gasped. "The pain grips my insides. It was bearable until I started to run."

"You should have told me."

"A warrior does not complain about personal discomfort." said Klud almost defiantly.

"But what has caused this?" Parrish suddenly feared the worst and imagined that his friend had been beaten and suffered crippling, possibly fatal internal injuries.

"No food." Klud gasped as another spasm of pain wracked his body.

"Stomach cramps!" said Parrish in realization. "When did you last eat?"

"Before I was taken." The Neolithic warrior remembered then that there were still many things his friend did not understand about the ways of Dannu's people. He would have smiled had he not been in so much pain, knowing it had to be explained to the great man. "They did not feed me Parrish because it would be a waste of food. I was only kept to bring you. Once you were in their hands they would kill me."

"And you knew this when you let them take you?"

"Yes."

Parrish was astounded. He couldn't decide whether Klud did what he did because his Chieftain had ordered it, or because he trusted in his friend to come and rescue him. He wouldn't insult the man either by asking him to clarify which reason it was but he now knew just how brave his Neolithic friend was and how far he was prepared to go on his word. All the way to the grave! He laid a hand almost tenderly on the man's shoulder.

"Klud." He said solemnly. "You have more bottle than anyone I have ever met."

In translation the word 'bottle' came out as 'pot' and the smaller man didn't understand.

"Huh?" He frowned at his Chieftain, who smiled down at him in the soft moonlight.

"You are truly the bravest man I have ever known." There was no real way of showing his appreciation. "And I am honoured to be your Chieftain." It was the best accolade he could think of.

This time Klud managed a grin. Parrish grinned back, helped his friend to his feet and, supporting him with his free arm, the two warriors struggled on down the hillside until they reached the cover of the woods in the valley bottom.

"Rest here." Parrish settled Klud against the trunk of a tree that offered an unobstructed view of the hillfort and, without another word, vanished into the night. The Neolithic man watched in the darkness, listening for any sounds of alarm from the village above him, but still everything remained quiet.

Parrish in the meantime had moved along the edge of the tree line until he found the giant oak he had originally set off from, and retrieved the bows and arrows. Returning once more to his friend he knelt close beside him and offered out the smaller of the two weapons.

"Here. I thought you might like this. It is very likely that we will need them soon."

Klud nodded and accepted his bow and quiver. The Chieftain seemed to think of everything.

"Do you think you can make it over the ridge?" Parrish thumbed over his shoulder at the hill behind them. "We need at least to get out of sight of Amaldach-bre."

It was quite a climb for a man in his condition but Klud nodded again.

Parrish grinned once more and helped him to his feet.

"I had hoped to go straight back to Dane-bre but that will not be possible with you like this. Once over the ridge though, I will cook us both some hot food. After you have eaten and rested we can be on our way, but we must be moving by the time the sun rises. They will be sure to come looking." He cast an eye up at the hillfort.

"Yes." agreed Klud. "I am sorry to slow you down my Chieftain."

"Do not be." He dismissed his friend's apology. "I did not know they would treat you so badly. Come. We must be gone from here. Once they discover that you have escaped, we will both be running for our lives."

Klud looked for a moment at his tall companion. His first instinct was to shun the idea of running away. A warrior should stand his ground and fight. But Parrish was Dannu's man and knew things no one else understood. He was proud to call himself friend to this man and trusted in his judgment, no matter how strange some of his decisions seemed to be.

Once more being supported by his Chieftain, a man who need not do any hard work, as was the right of the leader of a village, Klud was helped up the wooded hillside as together they headed for the brow above them, all the time aware that at any moment a cry might go up from inside the hillfort and then they would feel the hot eyes of enemies on their backs.

At last out of sight of Amaldach-bre, on the lee side of the ridge of Cranbourne Chase, Parrish set his friend down then proceeded to unpack equipment from his webbing while Klud watched in fascinated silence, his pain momentarily forgotten.

Parrish had deliberately saved what had been left of his military rations for an emergency and this, he decided, was certainly an emergency. Pulling various pieces of kit from the pouches around his midriff he bent to work. He set up his hexamine stove, opening it to reveal the remaining four fuel blocks inside. In his large mess tin he put some of the sun dried jerky, a generous helping of water, and the contents of the vegetable soup sachet. It only took moments to light the fuel blocks using a match from the little book of them that is part of the sundries pack inside all Army issue ration packs, before placing the de-hydrated meat and vegetable stew on the stove to heat and reconstitute. Next he gave Klud a small amount of water in the plastic cup of his 58 pattern drinking system, telling the smaller man to take lots of small sips and not to gulp it down. Giving the warming soup an occasional stir, he readied the smaller mess tin to go straight onto the heat once the soup was warmed through. The second oblong aluminium container held one of the famous British Army giant tea bags, some powdered milk and a lot of sugar all swimming around in cold water. It didn't look all that appetizing but Parrish knew both he and Klud were going to need all the energy they could get!

Klud was simply amazed at how quickly his friend could produce, light and cook hot food. Never had he seen it's like before. When Parrish at last offered him the rough and ready stew he eyed it for a second.

"Is it safe to eat?" It did not seem natural to make food so quickly in such unnatural conditions. Parrish laughed and scooped a spoonful into his mouth. He chewed for a few seconds then swallowed noisily, cocking one eyebrow.

"Not bad, considering I knocked it up in double quick time."

Klud didn't fully understand the words but ate. If it was good enough for his Chieftain, then it was more than good enough for him. Parrish put the tea on to boil and watched as his friend ate greedily, knowing that if they lived through the next few days they would not eat solid food again during that time. Apart from tea, and he was loath to use up every single tea bag he possessed, the only real sustenance they might get would be from beef drinks made from the two oxo cubes he still carried. And then only if they had time to light a fire to heat the water.

Almost exactly as the tea began to boil the last of the fuel blocks burned away to a dull orange flame before finally going out. They were the last and Parrish felt a sharp pang of sadness. One more small but none-the-less significant link with his future gone forever. He shared the tea equally between them. Klud turned his nose up at the strong, hot fluid.

"It tastes strange." He said.

I've tasted worse, thought Parrish, but not much.

"Yes, but it will make you strong. Drink." Klud drank. "We will rest until just before dawn, then we must go and go fast. The warriors of Amaldach-bre will be after us as soon as they find you missing, but I do not think that will be before the dawn."

"They will indeed come." agreed Klud. "Their Chieftain will be very angry. I could see that he was a strong leader. It will be a great insult to him."

Parrish took the description 'strong' to mean tyrannical but before he could find out more Klud asked. "Do we go straight back to Dane-bre now? If we travel as fast as when you came for me, we can be safely back inside the village within a day."

Parrish shook his head. Klud was in no fit state to travel fast. In fact he doubted that anyone could travel as quickly across the countryside as he had done the previous day. No, they would instead have to rely on stealth and evading tactics to avoid the pursuers from Hambledon Hill. In a straight race they would soon be run to ground.

"I can only move that fast when I am alone." He said, hoping that his friend would not question him further. Klud knew what he meant. When Dannu's man was alone with his mistress, there was no place beside them for mortal man. He never spoke, just listening as Parrish continued. "We must move in a direction that they would not expect. Perhaps then we can gain some distance and avoid them. We will try to get back to Dane-bre by a longer, less obvious path."

"They will track us." It was the unavoidable truth.

"I know, but we must keep ahead of them as long as possible.

Until you can move faster and we can out run them. Besides, I know a few tricks that might slow them down a bit." Klud considered for a few moments then nodded.

"Which way then my Chieftain?" he asked finally.

Parrish pointed away almost due east as the false dawn began to show, the rapidly receding darkness at their backs. It would very soon be morning.

"We go like the clappers towards the New Forest, mate." he said in English.

Although it would not be called 'the New Forest' for another fifty five centuries, Parrish knew where he meant and besides, he knew no other name for the area. He hoped also that it would turn out to be not so different from the place he used to camp in as a boy all those years ago, in the far distant future.

Klud cocked his head at the strange mumbo-jumbo words the Chieftain used on occasion. No one else knew what they meant but all understood that they were always powerful words. He just nodded sagely and watched as Parrish began to quickly pack away his kit.

The Chieftain of Amaldach-bre was indeed very angry on being informed of the escape of his prisoner and the loss of one more trophy. No sooner had the sun began to show above the distant horizon when he was woken from his slumbers to receive the bad news.

He stamped out into the chill air and listened with undisguised fury as the situation was explained to him. It was a report to make any commander furious. One of his men killed and in the centre of the village too, the holy man struck down and the main gate simply left standing ajar. The village shaman was brought before him, making his way through the parting crowd of gathering warriors who had been turned out of their own beds and told to go to the Chieftains hut at once.

The man they all faced waited impatiently, glowering at the dishevelled, still half asleep men before him. The steadily growing gathering had fallen silent when the holy man had arrived and passed among them to stand before their leader.

Even the Chieftain was briefly taken aback as everyone stared at the much respected man with his already swollen, disfigured lower jaw and split bottom lip. His still swelling face was beginning to turn a dark shade of blue along the jaw line, the colour spreading slowly up into his cheek. Who would dare to attack a holy one?

"Well?" The demand for an explanation burst from the Chieftains lips.

"It was the tall one called Parrish." slurred the shaman, not wanting to move his mouth any more than was necessary. There was a murmur of recognition from the gathered warriors. They all remembered the strange one from the great gathering at the Sanctuary the previous year. The murmurs were cut short by more harsh words from the Chieftain.

"Alone? Just one man?" he asked incredulously. "And what were all my brave warriors doing while this one man simply walked into the village, took what he wanted and then left, unnoticed let alone unchallenged?" The raw scorn in his voice made all the men before him bow their heads in shame.

The shaman was about to explain that Parrish was not just any man, but Dannu's man. He didn't get the chance. The Chieftain dismissed him with an insulting, brief wave of the hand and addressed his warriors.

"Get your weapons and be at the gate shortly. We will quickly track them down and kill them." he barked.

There was a moments silence and no one appeared to want to move. A warrior at the front of the crowd asked timidly.

"How many of us, my Chieftain?"

"All!" Shouted the irate man and stepped quickly up to the warrior, back handing him across the mouth, the slap sounding loud in the still morning air.

"Do not dare to question me, just do as I say! Every man who can use a weapon will come with me. These men cannot have gone very far and they must die for their insult. I will not have it, do you all understand?!"

He was shouting now, his face bright red with anger, fists clenching and unclenching in fury. All the warriors just nodded in agreement with their raging leader.

"Then go and make ready!" he screamed and turned his back on them all, stamping back into his hut to get his own equipment.

One of his wives, unfortunate enough to be in his way as he entered, was sent crashing violently back against the side wall of the hut by a sweeping forearm as he cleared his path.

10

The tall twentieth century man and his shorter Neolithic friend had by now set off into the false dawn, Klud still clutching at his tortured stomach. To his consternation the pains seemed to have become worse since he had eaten, not better.

Parrish took the lead, trying to draw his struggling companion on as quickly as he could without actually chivvying him along either physically or verbally. He was well aware that in his position as Chieftain, biting words towards this man who took his speeches as gospel would be more damaging than effective. Plus, from exhaustive Army fitness training exercises when he had been pushed to his limits, he knew what was coming. Sure enough, they had not travelled all that much farther when Klud's shrunken, strangled stomach finally rebelled and he retched up much of what he had eaten earlier.

Spitting the last of the vomit from his mouth and wiping his lips with the back of one hand, he apologized to his Chieftain for the loss of control. Parrish wasn't at all surprised at the reaction, just sorry for the waste of the solid food. All he had left now was a few pieces of jerky. He waved away the apology and patted his friend reassuringly on the back.

"No matter. The hot tea will still have helped you some and we may yet have the chance to make more hot food before the men of Amaldach-bre learn which way we have gone."

Klud smiled at the encouraging if not very truthful words and they moved off once more across the lower land towards the next gently sloping ridge a few kilometres ahead of them.

At valley bottom the pair came to a small, fast flowing and shallow stream. The merrily babbling water was crystal clear and a welcome sight. Both men drank then Parrish refilled his water bottle while Klud splashed the reviving wetness onto his face. As Parrish reached into the water he suddenly noticed the dark lines of camouflage cream still smeared across the backs of his hands and realized that he was still cammed up for night exercises. Bottle filled and safely stowed away in his webbing, the soldier washed his face and hands vigorously and with military thoroughness, removing all traces of the thick cream from his skin. Sitting back and drying himself with a sleeve he found his warrior friend smiling at him. Parrish raised his eyebrows in question.

"I was wondering when you would remove your strange battle paint." Klud explained. "Have you kept it on so that we might remain invisible to our enemies longer?"

Parrish laughed. He knew Klud had seen him once before in the dark, blacked up to prevent being seen in the night. He could understand how his simple friend might believe that such paint could give him the power of invisibility. Indeed, in the twentieth century much thought, research and experimentation had been put into military camouflage paint, producing a specifically designed product that's sole aim was to make a soldier blend in with the landscape and be difficult to see. The sudden thought of the last time he was blacked up reminded him of the tragedy of his wife and his laugh died as quickly as it had lived. He shrugged in answer to the question.

"I could not say, but it must be worth a try." There seemed no point in lowering his friend's morale any more than necessary. Besides, it was nice to still be something of a man of mystery to his people, even after living amongst them for more than two years.

If only he knew how they really thought towards him.

Klud poised a moment to consider his Chieftains words and Parrish, not wanting to waste any more time than necessary, clapped his friend on the shoulder, gave him a positively gestured thumbs up, then splashed quickly across the shallow stream to the other side. Klud frowned for a brief moment then tentatively copied his friend's action and also gave the thumbs up. Perhaps it was some mysterious and meaningful earth sign, he wondered? Then he too crossed the water and they set off once more.

The Chieftain of Amaldach-bre paced impatiently back and forth behind his best trackers while they searched valiantly for any sign of the two fugitives. They of course wished to please their leader with a quick result and a positive lead on the escapees, not to mention wishing to avoid his wrath any further. All the other warriors of the hilltop village watched and waited in silent trepidation further back behind their still irate Chieftain, every man there also wishing the trackers swift success.

It was not to be. The sun had risen steadily into the sky and the massed band of heavily armed warriors were being led a slow and frustrating path towards the north by the ever searching trackers. And still there were no signs.

Finally, one tracker accepted the inevitable and reluctantly approached his glowering leader.

"I am sorry my Chieftain but there are just no signs. None at all. I am sure that the two we seek have not passed this way."

"Pah!" Shouted the Chieftain and pushed the man roughly away. "Why did you not tell me earlier?" He turned back to face his hillfort village in the middle distance, staring away at it over the heads of all his warriors. It was as if he did not even see them but they still instinctively cringed beneath his livid eyes. He was indeed still furious but now he had had time to think. Slowly scanning the panoramic view spread out before him, he methodically considered the limited options that his prey were offered. If they had not headed straight back towards their own village, then which way had they gone?

It was most unlikely, he reasoned, that the men had headed westward. That way would clearly hold nothing for them as they travelled ever further away from their village. No help or sanctuary there, just a certain death, be it from when his warriors finally ran them to ground in the great forests or they were unfortunate enough to stumble across some other, just as hostile village. The same also for the south, although there were no known villages in that direction. Just the common rumour of a great lake of undrinkable water. It was also rumoured that if a warrior should stand at its edge, he would be unable to see the far shore, so great was this lake. Even if it were possible to cross this immense barrier, what then lay on the other side? No, he was sure they did not go to the south. Then all that remained was the east.

The Chieftain knew that the game was not so plentiful there, as did everyone else. It was only sparsely wooded and so his hunting parties did not travel too far in that direction. But, and the more he considered it the clearer it became, he realized that it was very possible that the two men might use this well known fact against him to throw him off their scent. He could see it all now. Once they were sure that he had been tricked and gone off in the wrong direction, it would be easy for them to head once more towards the north-west, hoping that they had put enough distance between themselves and Amaldach-bre's warriors to return safely to their own village.

The Chieftain cursed the valuable morning that he had wasted searching in the wrong direction, but all was not lost. He had uncovered their plot too soon. They must have thought him stupid to be taken in completely by such a plan, clever as it was. Hah! For that they would pay because now they had played into his hands. He knew the one they called Klud was sick and would be unable to move quickly across the land. Now that he knew their route he could track and run them to ground in the middle of the wilderness where there was no chance of them getting any help.

Yes, he had wasted almost half a day but their trick had not worked and he could soon regain the lost distance. He suddenly felt a warm glow of satisfaction and silently congratulated himself for his cleverness. As he continued to eye the rolling countryside in the warming sunshine, concentrating now on the east, a sly smile finally played across his vexed features. Somewhere out there, beneath his hawk-like gaze, were two men, all alone and running for their lives. And it was his grim intention to end their flight in pools of blood. Yes, if he and his band moved quickly they could be close behind the two strangers by late the following morning.

"Hah!" He barked again and pounded a fist against his thigh. "They go that way." A finger aggressively stabbed the air, pointing off towards the south east. "Come, we will run them both to ground and slaughter them like animals. I shall have their heads hanging in my stall before the sun sets tomorrow."

His warriors sincerely hoped so and submissively followed their suddenly grinning leader as he led back the way they had come. Back towards Amaldach-bre.

Parrish and Klud were by now heading across the undulating countryside of Neolithic southern Dorset, with Parrish hoping to cross the river Avon by nightfall and Klud following blindly in his Chieftains footsteps.

The warrior trusted in his sometimes mysterious Chieftains judgment and sense of direction even though he had never been on this part of Dannu's land before. His stomach still pained him but Parrish had been right about his strange tasting hot drink. It had given him some new strength and, although it was a struggle, he managed to keep up with his tall friend's pace.

Parrish, consciously keeping the pace to an easy rate that he thought Klud could manage, had a completely different set of problems on his mind. They were by now being actively pursued, he was sure. Pursued by a fit, well armed and well motivated band of men whose sole intention was to snuff them out.

Themselves, on the other hand were only two, lightly armed, far from any assistance and hampered through sickness. It was only a matter of time before they were overhauled. And what happened then didn't bear thinking about. At their present pace it would take several days even to get near enough to Danebury to alert the village with a signal fire. He knew the only way to keep himself and his friend alive was to somehow hold off the men of Amaldach-bre with delaying tactics. To try and buy themselves enough time to make good their escape. He secretly doubted that they would live past the next few days.

He explained his reasoning's in simpler terms to Klud, who just nodded. He too could see that their deaths were not far away.

"We must slow them down." Parrish concluded. "Then perhaps we can complete the distance back to Dane-bre before they can catch us." He didn't like to say the word 'kill'.

"But how do we do this?" Klud shrugged, the great eyebrows shooting up. "We are few and they are so many."

It was not fear. Parrish did not for one moment doubt his friend's courage, it was simply a statement of the truth.

"Psychological warfare."

The words of course meant nothing to Klud. Parrish corrected himself. "What we must do is confuse, distract and frighten them."

Klud shook his head. After so long living with Dannu's people did he still not know that her warriors were not afraid?

"You cannot easily frighten these men." He put it as politely as he could to his Chieftain. "They are warriors and know that we are few. It would take much to put fear of us into these men."

"Not fear of us." Parrish said slowly. "Fear for themselves."

Klud's eyebrows shot up again but all Parrish gave by way of an explanation was a smile. It was not a happy smile.

Not long after the sun had peaked in the sky a cry went up in the valley below Amaldach-bre. Everyone dashed over to the tracker who had called from where he was kneeling beside a giant oak.

"I have their track." he said simply, looking up at his Chieftain. "They go that way."

"Yes." agreed the man slowly. "It is as I thought. They head towards where the sun rises. Good."

He arrogantly paid no more attention to the tracker, naturally expecting the man to lead off along the track. Without another word spoken the insulted warrior simply picked up his weapons and set off along the, to him glaringly obvious, trail. All the other warriors of his village were no more than a few paces behind.

Meanwhile, the men of Danebury had made slow if not steady progress through the forest. Parrish regularly checked his little survival compass to be sure of the direction, each time doing his best to keep it hidden from Klud. It wasn't because he didn't want his friend to see the gadget, but because to try and explain to him how it worked would have been nigh on impossible and to say 'you just wouldn't understand' would be to insult him.

Well aware of the blatant trail they were leaving in their wake, the pair moved through the great expanse of broadleaf woodland barely aware of the great trees that towered above them, stretching up towards the warmth and energy of the sun. Unaware that was until they came across a massive deadfall that blocked their immediate path.

What had caused it to fall, be it a lightning strike, high winds or simply old age, who could tell, but the pair had to physically climb up onto its great trunk to get over it.

The obvious thing to do would have been to walk around it but Parrish had an idea. After jumping lightly to the ground he told Klud to jump too. Not onto the ground however, but onto his own back. The Neolithic warrior was unsure at first but bowed to his Chieftains wishes and did as he was told. As he was piggy-backed away from the tree he could not contain his curiosity or refrain from voicing his discomfort at being as it were above his Chieftain, allowing him to do the hard work while he, the lesser man, rested.

"Why are you carrying me, Parrish? I am not that sick. You are my Chieftain and should not burden yourself like this. It is an insult."

"Do not concern yourself with my insult." Parrish smiled. "I carry you only because I am stronger. If it were the other way around you would carry me, and I would not be offended."

"But why carry me at all?"

"To confuse our enemies. Up to where we met the tree there were two sets of tracks. But beyond it there is now only one. Remember what I said? Confuse, distract and frighten. Even if it only takes them moments to learn what we have done, it will be extra moments that we have gained over them."

Klud pondered briefly on this, gradually seeing the wiseness of his Chieftains thoughts and the confusion of their pursuers and the time they might waste looking for a separate second track before picking up their trail once more. He chuckled.

"I begin to see, my friend." he said.

Parrish chuckled too, hitched his friend higher up onto his back and tried to pick up the pace a little before he would set Klud down again, yet still taking care not to exhaust himself too much. Five hundred meters or so ought to be enough, he decided.

The ruse did indeed confuse the pursuing band and their Chieftain gnashed his teeth in barely contained fury as he once more lost time. But not too much because if nothing else, he was an organizer of men. His band was many and he spread them out to look for the non-existent second track. After perhaps half an hour, although there was no concept of time measurement in Neolithic England, the true trail was once again picked up. Two men, still heading east.

Many of the less intelligent warriors didn't understand what had happened to the second man's tracks. Surely he could not float through the air?

None of the men were about to ask their leader this though and there were a few dubious mutterings about strange forces being at work. The Chieftain at first wasn't sure either, before he at last grasped the idea that one must have simply carried the other. And then he never explained it to the others to put their minds at rest. He was more concerned with the fact that it was becoming ever clearer that this hunt might not be as straight forward as he had expected.

"They are trying to trick us." was all he said by way of explanation. "But it will not work. Be on the lookout for more tricks but know this. We will not be stopped and I *will* have their heads, as Dannu is my witness." He raised his eyes to the heavens.

The sudden brightness of the clear sky, lancing down through the leafy boughs, made him blink and squint, his eyes unaccustomed to the glare after the soft half light of the shady forest floor. He couldn't be sure but, just for a moment, did a dark shadow pass across the face of the sun?

Shaking his head violently to clear his vision he signalled to his warriors and they set off in pursuit of their elusive prey.

11

Arriving at the next stream, the men from Danebury didn't cross it directly but traversed along its length, splashing up the watercourse and emerging from the water some distance upstream. Parrish was sure this trick must be old even in Neolithic times but still felt obliged to try. Every second gained might turn out to be precious if the end of their deadly race was close run. He knew their pursuers were steadily gaining, as did Klud, who said so.

"They draw ever nearer." He glanced over his shoulder at the innocent looking forest behind them. "I feel it."

"Me too, but we must go on. While we live there is always hope."

"Hope?"

"A Dane-bre warrior does not give up." Parrish put on his firmest voice.

He knew his struggling friend would never even consider surrender but felt a morale boosting talk was needed. "We will carry on to the last my friend but we are a long way from finished. If we can get in sight of Dane-bre, the rest of the village will come."

"The warriors of Amaldach-bre will still fight." Klud stated the obvious.

"Yes." Parrish had already wrestled with this fact, knowing that it meant that because of his actions of what now seemed a lifetime ago, some of his villagers, also his friends and people who trusted in his judgment, would soon die. He had let them down and now they would have to suffer for it. The thought caused him great pain. "It is true, and so it is our duty to knock some of the fight out of them."

This was more like the fighting talk Klud preferred to hear. Perhaps now was the time to stop running like women and do battle with their enemies.

"Do we wait for them and attack when they do not expect it?" he asked expectantly, at the same time inadvertently clutching at his midriff as another stab of pain gripped him.

"A good plan, my friend. But with one problem." Parrish smiled grimly, noticing the hastily masked movement. "We would die quickly and with no gain. We must stay alive to lead the fight." He patted Klud on the shoulder. "And even Dane-bre's best warriors are wise enough to know not to fight when the enemy is so many."

Klud smiled briefly at the complement and bowed to the superior judgment of his leader.

"You are indeed a wise man. I am proud you are my Chieftain and honoured to be your friend."

"Know this Klud." said Parrish in a serious tone. "There is no other man I would rather fight alongside and, if need be, die alongside. But I do not now intend to be killed. We have not yet come to the end of our path, my friend. Trust me on this."

There was a long moment of eye contact between the pair, each man firm on his friendship with the other, and then, without another word being spoken, they moved on.

Parrish continued to draw his warrior friend along, struggling to keep them both ahead of their pursuers until the chance came to gain a little more breathing space between them. Klud was still in a poor condition, a long way from fighting fit and badly needing something more inside him for sustenance. The only edibles that remained in Parrish's' pouches were strips of jerky and his oxo cubes. The jerky would probably do more harm than good to a dry and shrunken stomach, yet to heat water for a beef drink would take time. Valuable time. But there was a place. A place where they might gain the time needed to prepare.

On ahead of them, exactly how far ahead he wasn't sure, the river Avon crossed their path. It would be wider and deeper this far downstream from its source. Parrish knew from experience that to take a large group across a river, no matter how well the group were organized, would take time. If he and Klud crossed quickly they could use the gained time to rest briefly and heat some food, giving his struggling friend the chance for a respite and some much needed nourishment. There would also be the chance then to implement some of the more aggressive delaying tactics he had been considering. And so he coaxed his partner along. It was imperative that they reach this natural barrier ahead of the men of Amaldach-bre. Before they might be killed.

"Here." Parrish handed his MOD survival knife to Klud. "As we travel, cut down a few thin saplings and make me some wooden stakes. About as long as your forearm. Make sure they are well sharpened at one end."

"Weapons?" Klud only asked about their possible use, not for a moment questioning his Chieftains strange order.

"Yes," came the solemn reply. "Weapons to put fear into them." To terrify them, Parrish thought. Terrorist weapons. It was a matter of great distaste to him that he was now resorting to the very methods, using evil, cowardly and callously indiscriminate weapons that his entire army training had prepared him against. The kind of weapons against which there was no defence and permitted no retaliation. Those that struck without warning. Those used by people with no honour.

Klud simply nodded and set about his given task, occasionally shooting puzzled glances at his Chieftain, who was also busy, sorting out lengths of the strong green cord he carried in a tight bundle, as well as some of that thin, almost invisible thread that he called his fishing line.

The Chieftain of Amaldach-bre was in better spirits now. He moved up beside his lead tracker. It would be too much to expect the man to smile but even though he was nowhere near as skilled as the man by his side, it was still blatantly obvious to see that he and his warriors were closing steadily in on their prey.

"We draw ever closer, my Chieftain." said the tracker, as if reading the thoughts of his leader.

"Yes." There was a hint of grudging satisfaction in the gruff reply. "And the big river is not far ahead. If that slows them down even more, we might be with them by the setting of the sun." He squinted up at the hot orb now low in the sky above the forest, almost seeming to be impaled upon the tops of the trees.

The tracker just nodded in reply. There was nothing to be said.

At that moment Parrish was also gazing up at the sun, shielding his eyes with a raised hand. He had hoped to be across the river well before dusk but was now running out of time. Looking back down to the path ahead he bumped into Klud, who had stopped in front of him, a hand also raised but this time in request for silence.

"Wha ...?"

"Listen."

The two men fell silent, straining their ears. After a few moments of listening to the common, everyday sounds of the countryside, the faint, rushing tinkle of flowing water could just be made out.

"Yes!" Parrish ejaculated and punched his friend amicably on the shoulder. "We made it."

The significance of simply reaching one more stream was lost on Klud and he could not ask his friend to explain for Parrish had already dashed ahead, eager to seek out the source of the sound. The Neolithic man just shrugged, gathered up his armful of short staves and followed on as best as his physical condition would allow.

Finally reaching the river Klud looked on in dismay, a complete contrast to his Chieftains obvious joy. Parrish saw a simple river crossing ahead with perhaps an hour's relief waiting on the other side. Klud saw not just another stream but an almost impassable barrier, too deep to wade and too wide to jump.

In fact, the pair were standing on the riverbank not far south of where, in fifty five centuries time, the bridge that gave the Hampshire village of Fordingbridge its name would span the waters of the magnificent river Avon.

Perhaps Klud's assessment of the sight before them was more realistic than his tall friends. The water was perhaps five or six feet deep at its centre, even more in some places and a good forty metres of open, flowing waterway spanned the gap between the river's banks.

Parrish, unaware of his partner's unspoken worries, turned to face him and took the pointed shafts.

"I'll tie these up and lead across, you follow."

Klud now looked even more dismayed but Parrish did not notice, already bending to his task. It took but a few moments to complete. Then he unclipped his poncho roll and spread the waterproof out on the ground.

"OK, now take your clothing off."

Klud simply did as he was told. Shortly they were both completely naked and Parrish packed both sets of garments in the centre of the poncho along with the stakes. Next he bundled the whole thing up, making sure that all the open edges were uppermost.

"C'mon." was all he said and without looking back lead the way to the water's edge, wading carefully in until his impromptu flotation bag became buoyant. He held their bows and quivers on top of the makeshift swim aid and, with strong kicks, swam steadily out into the current, being carried a short way down stream before his feet once again found a purchase on the bottom near the far side. The cold sting of the water against his bare skin made him gasp yet was at the same time most invigorating. He waded ashore and unwrapped his poncho smiling in satisfaction. All the clothing was still dry.

"Good. Now then Klud I ..." He turned and stopped in mid sentence, surprised to see his naked friend still standing more than forty yards away on the far bank.

"C'mon." He beckoned him to cross. "It is easy and will make you feel good too."

Klud just shook his head. Parrish was very surprised then. Warriors simply did not say no to their Chieftain, even when it was just between friends and with no one else about.

"What is wrong?"

"I cannot." his friend called back.

Parrish clapped himself on the forehead in disbelief. Just his luck. When the chance comes to gain a little time and breathing space he finds himself lumbered with a partner who cannot swim.

He quickly admonished himself then for the grossly unfair thought. He could never be considered 'lumbered' with a friend as true as Klud. Then, considering it even more, the real truth dawned.

Of course Klud couldn't swim. It was very unlikely that anyone at all in Danebury could swim. Why should they? They would never need to. No one who lived there had probably ever seen water deep enough even to totally submerge in, let alone swim across.

"Wait there." He called somewhat unnecessarily and walked upstream along the bank until he was once again opposite his friend. With a bright splash he flat dived into the clear water and struck out for the far bank in a fast crawl.

He was a very proficient swimmer thanks to the well scheduled fitness training programs drawn up by the Light Infantry PTI's. It was their job to keep Her Majesties fighting men in good condition and battle ready at all times. Swimming was a good way to promote all round fitness and develop stamina. In less than a minute Parrish was once more standing, dripping before his friend. The warrior's look of trepidation had changed to one of complete amazement.

"How can you move across the water like that?" he asked, astounded. There was awe in Klud's voice. Had he just been permitted by the Earth Goddess to see another of her man's strange powers? "You did not sink. And I know it is not possible that a river can take a man's weight."

"It is called swimming." said Parrish dismissively. "And it was taught to me long ago."

Then the Neolithic man realized what was expected of him next. But he was just an honest warrior who walked on Dannu's land and knew he would always come a poor second to his great Chieftain, whose abilities went far beyond his own. Beyond any other mans. Yet there was still something he could do for his friend.

"I could never do that." Klud shook his head. "You must go on without me. I will hold them off here as long as I can while you return to Dane-bre."

Parrish was once more impressed with the unselfish bravery of his stalwart friend but had no intention of leaving him behind. But he too understood the man's dilemma. He could appreciate that Klud knew the simple fact that people died beneath the water and up till now he had never known of anyone who could stay on the top of it. This common knowledge would of course work to their advantage against the men of Amaldach-bre, but only if they themselves crossed quickly to make the most of it.

"We must cross and cross now." said Parrish firmly. "I will help you to the other side," he added before Klud could say anything, "but you must do exactly as I say."

His friend paused only briefly before nodding in agreement, although his apprehension was clearly evident in his eyes.

Together they entered the chill water and waded out until it was up to Klud's chest. Parrish turned his back on the flowing current and bid Klud do the same, stepping up close behind his smaller friend. He cupped one hand under the unresisting Neolithic man's chin.

"You must trust me now my friend." He said softly. "In a moment I will ask you to lay back into the water. Try to be at rest and breathe easily. Do not speak while we cross and do not be afraid." Parrish knew full well that if the man panicked while in mid stream it was most likely he would then drown, possibly dragging Parrish down with him too. Even so, he would not openly use the word panic to his companion for it would seem like an insult.

Klud took a few deep, nerve steadying breaths then nodded again. He was ready.

Parrish never understood that his friend would not panic, simply because he had unfailing faith in his great Chieftain. Despite the fact that Klud could not swim, knew that the water was deeper than he was tall and so death might be only a few feet away, he believed completely that he would not die, because his Chieftain was with him. And where his Chieftain went, so went Dannu.

"OK." was all Parrish said and slowly the pair lay back in the flowing water. "Just relax mate and it'll be a piece of cake." he added quietly in English and then he struck confidently out towards the far shore behind him. Supporting Klud's head clear of the water with the hand beneath his chin, a textbook water recovery technique, the tall man used strong leg kicks and a wide sculling action with his free hand to tow Klud out into mid stream.

Klud just floated, as relaxed as could be expected of a nervous man, trying to understand the strange sensations he now experienced. His body felt as if it had no weight. It was harder to breath with his Chieftains hand around his chin and occasionally water splashed onto his face and in his mouth. Yet he did not cough or make any other sound, not wishing to disturb his Chieftain while he used his strange powers. There were unknown forces at work here, he knew.

Parrish had uttered some more of his strange, unintelligible words just before they had started to cross, perhaps calling upon Dannu for help, for it totally baffled the Neolithic man how his friend managed to propel them both through something that a man could not push against or hold on to. Yes, he knew that the Earth Goddess was near at hand and, rather than being afraid, even while at the peril of his own life, he felt strangely proud that he was somehow allowed, almost privileged, to share for a brief time, Parrish's closeness with his mistress.

Suddenly Parrish jerked Klud upright and as the man slid down in the water and began to struggle, splashing against the dangerous waters, his feet found a purchase on the riverbed beneath him. He stood up and found himself no more than waist deep. They were across.

Parrish was breathing heavily but grinned as they waded out, more than satisfied with the relatively easy crossing.

"OK?" He asked cheerily.

To his surprise Klud turned and faced him, a very solemn look on his face and without uttering a word bowed very deeply. Puzzled, all Parrish could do was bow back. Then he clapped his friend on the shoulder and steered him towards where their clothes waited.

"Come on then, we have work to do."

12

After carefully choosing a campsite just inside the tree line near the river's edge, Parrish had Klud make a fire so they could boil some water for that badly needed hot drink. In order to get the fire going quickly it was helped along by Parrish plucking out two of the blank 7.62 rounds from the dozens that still bulged one of his front ammo pouches, prising the crimped ends open and sprinkling their contents onto it. The moment Klud's flint sparks produced a glowing ember in the little nest of tinder the charcoal grey gunpowder fizzled brightly into life, the tinder immediately bursting into flame. This of course astounded the Neolithic man, who quickly heaped on twigs, grasses and then larger pieces of dry, combustible timber to feed the flames. In no time at all a mess tin of clear river water was beginning to steam.

Klud wanted to ask his friend about the magic powder but Parrish said it would have to wait. Right now they had more important things to do. Right now they had to dig a number of small pits around their camp area. The two bent to their task and quickly dug out five square edged holes, each two feet square and a little less than two feet deep. Into the bottoms of each of these Parrish set a number of the stakes Klud had made, wedging them firmly into the hard earth, with their points uppermost. Then he covered the mouths of the holes with a thin layer of criss-crossing twigs and sprinkled this with loose soil, leaves and other matter from the forest floor. To the unpractised eye it was now difficult to see exactly where they were.

Klud had not seen their like before and cocked an eye at his

Chieftain.

"What do you hope to catch with these odd traps?" he asked.

"Their attention." replied Parrish gruffly before he set off alone into the trees to prepare another trap. It didn't take long to find what he wanted. A strong springy bough that stretched across a gap between the trunks at about waist height. To this he lashed the remaining sharpened stakes, drove pegs into the ground either side of his intended path as anchor points for the trip wire, then pulled the bough back until it was under great strain. He secured it in this position with some of his paracord, one end of it tied to the bough, the other linked to a length of his fishing line. The far end of this line was held gingerly in position where it was tied to a barb shaped tongue of wood that was hooked into a notch in the far side peg. The trip wire was held close to the ground by the other end, looped as it was around the near side ground peg. Touching the trip wire would dislodge the barb and release the straining bough, making it lash violently back across the path between the two pegs. It gave Parrish no satisfaction at the completion of such a complex booby trap. For that was indeed what it was. An evil device to kill or maim the unaware.

Back once more at the camp he stirred an oxo cube into the now boiling water and together the men shared the beefy, reviving brew.

"It tastes strange but is good." Klud commented.

"Yes. It will give you new strength. After you have drunk you might even try some more jerky."

Klud nodded and sipped some more. Then he looked again at his Chieftain and asked a question that had begun to bother him.

"These little traps ..."

"Punji pits." interrupted Parrish.

"They will not kill?"

"No. But they will badly injure and, more importantly, they will make the men of Amaldach- bre more wary of where they tread."

"I see." Klud understood.

"You do?" asked Parrish, a little surprised.

"To make them fear for themselves." The Neolithic man repeated the apparently prophetic words his Chieftain had spoken earlier.

He did indeed understand and suddenly Parrish felt sad. Sad that he had somehow, in a small way, polluted Klud's clear mind with dark drop of deviousness and unnecessary cruelty.

"You must tell no one of these things." He pointed to the covered pits around them. "They are bad and I only use them to keep us alive longer."

Klud simply nodded once more. He never tried to understand his tall friends reasoning's but would of course obey his Chieftains wishes. Besides, he quickly dismissed any thoughts of the pits from his mind as he concentrated once more on the strange but wonderful drink. It was most reviving. The more he drank the better he felt. Parrish let his friend have the bulk of the brew, pleased that he kept it down and was further gratified when the little man slowly ate a couple of pieces of jerky too. One small victory at least.

By now the sun was very low in the sky, glinting between the trunks of the forest, seeming to wink at the men as breeze blown leaves waved in front of it.

The two men set off once more into the trees. They left the glowing embers of their fire to be seen by their pursuers, a light to attract the moths to the flame, and their blatantly obvious tracks led towards the twentieth century man's other deadly surprise. At that site Parrish removed the leafy branch he had thrust into the ground there as a marker, carefully steered Klud around the booby trap then lead again, only going on a short distance before changing direction and heading north. North towards Danebury. In perhaps half an hour or so it would be dark and then the pace would become very slow. But he hoped his deadly rear guard would slow down the others too. At least until the morning. He had an awful feeling that the coming morning would probably be their last.

If he ever found out, it would have surprised Parrish to know that for all his efforts, the most successful barrier against the men who hunted him was actually the river itself.

In driving his men across it without proper preparations, the Chieftain of Amaldach-bre made his first big mistake. It cost him several of his men.

He had his scouts quickly check a short way up and down the riverbank and they soon found a place where it was possible for a man to cross. Barely. If he was careful. Here the river was just about shallow enough for a Neolithic warrior not to submerge fully, the water rising up to chin height. But the river still flowed relentlessly and the crossing was to prove a real test of nerve.

For moral support the warriors crossed as a group, bunching too closely together. What happened next was almost inevitable. While in mid-stream one man lost his footing on the pebble strewn, weed entangled riverbed. He stumbled and plunged beneath the surface, suddenly robbed of the life giving air. Grabbing wildly at the man next to him in a vain attempt at recovery he dragged that unfortunate down too, the pair gasping, gagging and fighting wildly but ineffectively against the unyielding, undefeatable flow of the river. This triggered a blind panic and a wild, splashing stampede to gain the safety of the bank.

By the time all the surviving, wet, wild eyed warriors stood once more on firm ground, water dripping from their chins onto their heaving chests, the Chieftain of Amaldach-bre knew there were men missing. He could not be sure how many, and it was an indictment to his callousness that he never tried to find out exactly who was missing, but some of the men who stood before him had suddenly lost a friend or a relative.

The Chieftain did not know the death toll for he could not count, but further downstream where the Avon swept into a wide, shallower, gravel bottomed bend, the limp, lifeless bodies of six of his warriors were already beginning to drift slowly towards the bank, coming in gently and grounding face down on its shingle bank.

Back among the living, there were low grumblings from the men that perhaps this hunt was now not such a good thing. Perhaps Dannu was not with them. Could two men be worth so much to their Chieftain? Although they would not say so out loud, the men were all for returning to their homes. But their leader would have none of it. He was even more incensed at the increasing costs in men, not to mention his loss of face and personal standing with his warriors, that the two he now hunted were inflicting upon him. With gritted teeth he ordered his band on and they of course followed. Followed their Chieftain towards the faintly glowing embers of a small campfire. One that glittered invitingly out from among the darkening shadows cast by the failing light of the dusk.

Parrish and Klud both froze momentarily in their tacks as a high, agonized cry rang suddenly out through the night. The traps had found a victim and the man who had organized then closed his eyes, his spirit sinking a little lower. There was no elation in knowing that the pits, or at least one of them, had worked successfully. He knew it had been necessary but that it was also not an honourable thing to do and, now that the deed was done, as he weighed one reason against the other, he found himself wishing he'd never dug the damned things and had settled for some more honourable approach to what was almost certain to end in their eventual if not imminent deaths.

Klud on the other hand just saw the obvious and commented on it.

"They are very close, my Chieftain. We must move more quickly or they will catch us during this night. It will be hard to fight them in the darkness."

"Yes." Parrish admired the man's ability to just see the smaller picture and not have his mind clouded by twentieth century guilt and conscience. "But they will tread more slowly now, or at least for a while, in fear of more pits. And they will have injured men now too. This will also slow them down."

The Neolithic man looked up at his friend's face, trying to make out the strong features in the rapidly diminishing light. Did he really believe the words he spoke or was he just trying to cheer himself up? For two summers now the tall man had lived among the people of Dannu's land and yet still it seemed he did not always understand them.

"But Parrish, surely you must know that if those who fall into our pits are too badly hurt to keep moving, they will be quickly killed. It is the only way."

"Oh, God." gasped Parrish quietly in English. For all his planning and scheming to delay the men of Amaldach-bre he had forgotten the savage truth of these times and it suddenly horrified him. If an injury was so severe as to render a person incapable, even if the injury was one it was possible to eventually recover from, then the people here considered the injured party too great a liability, a drain on their already scant resources, and so the injured one was ritually killed.

"Do not look so sad, my friend." Klud clapped him on the arm. "It will make the hunting part less in size. Not so many for us to kill when the time comes." He offered his Chieftain a toothy grin, lost in the gathering darkness.

Parrish just stared back at the shadowy figure of his friend. The drink and small amount of solid food was certainly beginning to work on his Neolithic partner. He seemed to be feeling better by the minute. He wished he could say the same for himself.

"You are right, my friend." He returned the clap on the arm. "And yes, we must keep moving. Dane-bre is still more than a day's walk away to the north. Perhaps we can still reach the safety of our village before these men can catch us."

With the pursuing band less than an hour behind them it was a forlorn hope, he knew, but Klud nodded enthusiastically, secure in his faith of the righteousness of his Chieftain. The warrior led off in the direction indicated by his Chieftains pointing finger, while Parrish followed more sullenly behind, trying not to think of the agonies his traps were now inflicting on those innocent yet determined men whose sole intent was to see them dead.

Against Parrish's expectations, the punji pits did not have any particularly detrimental effects on the morale of the warriors of Amaldach-bre.

True, when the unfortunate victim of one pit fell screaming to the ground, his foot and ankle wrecked by the vicious trap, the other men froze in their tracks, warily eyeing the ground around them. But the experienced trackers of the group, expert in reading the tell tale signs on the floor of the great forest, soon spotted the locations of the other pits, only hastily camouflaged. The camp area was soon made safe. The men even watched with an almost detached disinterest as the injured man was swiftly killed. He was judged by the Chieftain to be beyond help and his execution order was carried out without qualm.

It was the second, more elaborate trap that put new fear into the hearts of the warriors of Amaldach-bre. With the light now virtually gone it was impossible to see the traps actuating mechanism, namely the trip wire. The man who fell victim to it was struggling against the encroaching darkness to get a few final glimpses of their prey's tracks, doing his best to ascertain their continuing direction, before it was completely dark. He led the warrior band along in his familiar crouching, occasionally bowing stance that denoted a tracker at work as his eyes strained towards the ground. His dedication to his craft was admirable and the Chieftain of Amaldach-bre thought his lead tracker the most skilful woodsman he had ever seen.

The trackers last thought was one of puzzlement. He was baffled that the tracks seemed to completely disappear, just for a moment. As he took his final, fatal step forward, bending forward once more in an attempt to confirm his thoughts, one foot snagged the invisible fishing line. The trap sprung.

Because of his stooping posture, the bough swept in just beneath the man's chin and took him fully across the chest, the stakes driving right through the body cavity, their points punching bloodily out through the back of his buckskin tunic. The tracker died without uttering a single sound, suddenly just hanging there from the bough that now sagged under the dead weight impaled upon it.

Everyone was shocked, even the Chieftain. The whole thing had happened in the blink of an eye and no one could understand how. How could a man die so suddenly when there appeared to be no danger near at hand? And how did a simple tree branch know just when to strike? Clearly Parrish and his warrior friend must have made the trap but they were known to be some distance away. Close enough to soon be caught but plainly too far off to have let the branch go themselves.

There were fresh grumblings from the warriors now, barely concealed from the ears of their Chieftain. Unanswerable questions raced between the worried men, stoking up the fires of fear now beginning to burn within them. Was the forest itself now turning against them? Was there any truth in the wild rumour that the tall one might be Dannu's man? They had of course heard the whispered stories at the great Gathering, but it had all been nothing but idle women's gossip. Or had it?

The men had seen how she had allowed the two easy and safe passage across the wide river and now it looked like the land itself, Dannu's land, was beginning to fight them. They had now lost many men to the realm of Dannu during this ill fated chase. Was their pursuit of the two right in the eyes of the Earth Goddess?

Yet still their crazed Chieftain ordered his men forward once more. Unable to count the losses among his men, the eight casualties totalling almost a quarter of his warrior force, he was unwilling to listen to the fears and discontentment of his men. He would not have accepted their reasoning's because he had all but lost his own. In his eyes he had now lost great face, lost many men and had had his integrity, and that of his entire village, destroyed. Destroyed by just two men. All he had left now was his thirst for revenge. These men must pay with their lives.

"They are now but a short distance ahead." he growled through grinding teeth. There was no longer any need for him to shout. The quiet, savage menace that bordered on insanity was cuttingly evident in his tone. "We will have them shortly after first light tomorrow. This task I will have done. Then and only then can we all return home to celebrate our victory and honour our dead."

The men knew they could not disagree with their chosen leader and sullenly agreed, clinging onto the one cheery thought offered to them. Just one more day and this nightmare chase would be over.

13

Now that they had crossed the river, Parrish knew he was in the New Forest proper, but had little time to revel in returning to the land of his distant childhood. The pair climbed the ridge that rose up a short way off from the eastern side of the Avon, on its brow passing without being aware of it over the site where a small and somewhat insignificant hillfort called Frankenbury would one day be built. Then they headed north, Parrish checking his little button compass, eyes more concerned with that than the immediate surroundings. There was nothing much to see in the dark anyway. One section of forest appeared to be much like another.

The pace was painfully slow and fraught with anxiety. Neither of the two groups could speed up for fear of risking injury by stumbling about in the night. Parrish and Klud knew that any injury meant slowing down which in turn would lead to capture and death. The men of Amaldach-bre feared the prospect of more of the tall man's Dannu traps but could not stop in case their prey drew away from them. It was a tense, drawn out night and although very few actual kilometres were covered across the undulating ground, to the men of the chase, both hunters and hunted, it felt like they had crossed half of all Dannu's land. Both groups were relieved to see the glow of the false dawn slowly turn the trees to silhouettes against the lightening sky, the fatigue of two sleepless nights etched in every face.

As the sun rose Klud looked to his Chieftain. He knew they had gained nothing on their pursuers, who were no more than a short distance behind, and hoped that the tall man might have one more trick to delay them If not, they might die this very day.

Parrish was thinking the same thoughts and deliberately avoided his friends attempted eye contact. He stared out over the now revealed landscape, trying to pick out some landmark he might remember from his youth. He could not. Although it was still the Forest, with its large stands of both spruce and broadleaf trees interspersed with many small clearings, there seemed to be a lot more trees than he remembered and of course there were none of the fenced enclosures. He had hoped his familiarity with the land here might aid him in evading the pursuing group but it was not to be. Parrish too knew that they would die this day, still more than a day's walk from home.

The depleted men of Amaldach-bre were glad to see the coming of the day. As the sun crept up over the horizon the strain and relief was clear on their faces. This was to be the last day of this ill fated chase. Today it would finish and they could all return to their homes. The men looked once more to the Chieftain who led them. There was no longer the eagerness to listen to and obey his wishes that they once felt. Everyone knew he had made bad choices and done things that were not right. Dannu was surely watching and the men began to wonder if she would bring her wrath down upon the man who was close to offending the great Earth Goddess. The man in question could feel the hostile eyes on his back. He knew he had pushed his men almost as far as they would go. But all he had now was his hate for the two men ahead of him. Especially the tall one called Parrish. If he could catch and kill them swiftly he would both satisfy his thirst for revenge and, with the taking of their heads, have his honour and that of his village restored to him. He would of course kill the tall one himself if it were possible, but once they were both dead his men would once again respect him and the village of Amaldach-bre could return to some semblance of normality.

But the Chieftain needed something now to carry his group that last step to the final conflict. They were very reluctant now, he knew. Just then, as if in answer to his silent call, on the skyline no more than a kilometre ahead the two they chased rose briefly into view, cresting the low ridge.

"See!" he shouted, pointing dramatically. "There they are. We are so close now. Let us go fast and we shall have their heads very soon."

His men saw the distant figures move furtively out of sight and their spirits lifted. Lifted at the prospect of an even quicker end than expected. They all nodded in agreement and moved quickly on, almost at the run. The killing time was very near.

Parrish and Klud poised and looked back into the valley behind them. There, not too far away, emerging from the last tree line, were the men who pursued them. They seemed relentless. Unstoppable.

"Shit!" cursed Parrish and together he and Klud hurried on towards the next cluster of huge oaks and into the denser forest beyond.

The pursuing pack were closing rapidly now. Ahead of them the men from Danebury had just crossed a grassy clearing in the middle of this particular wood. The open space was no more than thirty meters across, an irregular circle of bright, sunlit meadow within the shady forest. A woodland butterfly alighted gently on one of the many clusters of bright woodland flowers that spotted the quiet glade and somewhere nearby a bird chirped merrily. The place was peaceful and serene.

And soon to be a killing ground.

Just as the pair reached the far side of the clearing the men of Amaldach-bre emerged unseen into the sunlight.

The first, too hastily fired arrow passed between Parrish and Klud and embedded itself with a thud into the tree just ahead of them. In a natural reaction, Klud turned to see where the arrow had come from. Parrish didn't hesitate, his Army training coming to the fore, and hurled himself at his partner, bringing them both crashing to the ground. Several more arrows passed right where the Neolithic man had been standing scant moments before, whooshing harmlessly on to be lost in the woods. The two men scrambled to their feet and darted swiftly for the protection of the nearest trees, more arrows punching into the ground around them. Reaching the temporary safety offered in the shelter behind the broad, brown trunks, Klud looked across at his friend, crouching down behind a great oak only a few feet away. He realized that his life had just been saved and wanted to offer his thanks, but Parrish was busy nocking his first arrow to the great bow. The kind words would have to wait and the smaller warrior did likewise and began to return fire. Arrows crossed the bright clearing, launched from both camps, burying their keen edged heads almost energetically into the trees on the opposite side.

It was a stalemate that could only last for a short time. Shots had to be exchanged on a regular basis. The men of Amaldach-bre making sure that their prey did not slip away into the woods and the men of Danebury doing their best to keep their pursuers at bay. But Parrish and Klud had less than a dozen arrows between them and it did not take long before all Parrish's black arrows were gone. Klud knew he could use Amaldach-bre arrows if any fell within his reach, but they alone would never be enough. With both their quivers now empty, that was it. The game was up and the deadly race was finally run.

Klud looked across at his Chieftain once more. He was not afraid, just disappointed. Disappointed that they had not survived. For they had done no wrong and the Neolithic man suddenly felt the Earth Goddess had let them both down. He had all the time expected to make it home safely, secure in the knowledge that he partnered Dannu's man and that she always smiled on him. But not now it seemed. He never dreamed that she would abandon her man and leave him to his fate but now, and he knew there was no alternative, they were both about to die. It seemed the Earth Goddess had closed her eyes to their troubles and left them to their doom. Klud's jaw set in a firm line. Yes, he would die now, but not for the honour of Dannu. His allegiance now was to his friend.

At that moment Parrish stood up behind his arrow studded tree, deftly unstrung his bow and rested it carefully against the trunk. He then drew his knife, gripping it tightly in his fist. Klud understood. He tossed his own bow aside and pulled from his tunic belt the prized, polished stone battle axe. They eyed each other for a long moment. Truer friends there had never been, each man solid with his trust and faith in the other. It was time. Then Parrish stepped boldly out into the open.

At that moment a single arrow, launched by some unknown warrior opposite, flew straight and true across the little clearing. Everything seemed to slow down as each and every man there watched in silent fascination as the missile completed its short flight. Almost without sound it lanced through the sunlight and struck Parrish, thudding hard into his midriff. Klud stared in horror as the unthinkable happened.

Parrish felt the impact and just looked blankly down at the offending arrow. Strangely, his first thought was of how well it had been made. The lethal implement was stuck, wedged hard into the front of his left ammo pouch, the one full of blank rounds. The flint head had not even pierced through to his combat jacket, pulled tight behind the belt that held the pouch. For a long moment there was total silence as all watched the tall man, looking down at the arrow who's deadly strike he seemed somehow impervious to. To everyone's amazement Parrish reached out and grasped the shaft, snapped it off leaving just a stub of dowelling apparently sticking out from his body, and threw the broken arrow aggressively to the ground. He looked at Klud, grinned a cold smile that sent a shiver down the smaller man's spine then nodded. Klud understood, nodded back and as one they raised their weapons in the air, yelled at the top of their voices and charged off across the clearing towards the slack jawed warriors of Amaldach-bre.

It was a magnificent but futile gesture. Both knew they would never reach the other side. By the time they approached the middle of the clearing their cries were fading and the men opposite had recovered their composure. They all stepped clear of cover and drew back their short bows to shoot down the two friends long before they could get within arm's reach.

The soft, deadly whoosh of arrow sound once more filled the air. The two from Danebury winced in anticipation of multiple arrow strikes but to their surprise arrows came not towards them but from behind them, arcing over their heads and into the now exposed group of Amaldach-bre warriors. Several fell to the volley and the two at the centre of it all stopped in their tracks, stunned, and turned to see where the mysterious missiles had come from. Their turning coincided with a return volley from the Amaldach-bre camp and for a staggering third time arrows passed by Klud and Parrish without either one being hit. They passed on and into the very large group of men now charging out of the same trees that not long before had protected the two.

A few from this third party fell to the arrows as they ran and then they were with Parrish and Klud, passing swiftly by with blood curdling cries, and on into vicious hand-to-hand combat with the men of Amaldach-bre. One of the passing men stopped briefly and grasped the astounded pair by their shoulders.

"Come on!" yelled Gant excitedly. "There are trophies to be taken!" With that he too charged off into the melee, swinging his flint headed axe above his head with much gusto.

Parrish and Klud faced each other, for a moment oblivious to the death struggles going on just a few feet away, laughed out loud with joy and relief, then together spun on their heels and joined the rest of the men of Dane-bre in the fight.

It was all but over even before they got there. The warriors of Amaldach-bre, their numbers already decimated during the pursuit and by Parrish's traps and schemes, were well outnumbered by the full complement and well motivated warriors of Danebury.

Those that were previously hunters now became easy prey for the massed warriors who fell hungrily upon them. Hungry for trophies, prestige and battle honours. Yet those about to die fought bravely. With honour.

Tomps, young and fast, was one of the first in. He used the dodging tactic copied from his Chieftain and perfected in another battle, to feign away from an attacking blow and in return took his opponent through the base of the throat with his axe. Narn too claimed a trophy, crashing head on with his opposite in the more traditional way of Neolithic war. In fact, Tomps was the only man of the times, apart from Parrish himself, who had any concept of evasive close quarters combat manoeuvres to gain an advantage against an opponent. In contrast to Tomp's skill, Narn used brute force. He and his 'chosen' man of Amaldach-bre both jarred with the impact, their war clubs locked together as they fell. The Danebury man was simply faster to regain his feet and struck down the slower man as he was getting up.

But the fight was by no means a one sided contest. Although the twenty or so Amaldach-bre men faced close to forty from Danebury, they still claimed a few of their own victims. Yet those that struck down their primary attackers achieved only a slight reprieve, more opposing warriors simply doubling up on the next attack to overpower these more hardened fighters.

Then it was over. Men lay dead or dying all along the edge of the clearing. Parrish gritted his teeth against the awful sight and let his men do what was always done after a battle. They passed among the bodies to finish off any injured men and to collect their grisly trophies.

It did not take too long and they began to gather before their

Chieftain, those clutching heads in one hand grinning even more than the rest, who were as gleeful to see the surprised but relieved look on their leaders face as they were of their battle victory. Klud, who had also quickly walked among the dead, pushed to the front of the crowd and said disappointedly,

"My Chieftain. Their own Chieftain is not among them." He had a personal score to settle with the man but that now took second place. There was a long moment before he could bring himself to say the dirty words. "He left his warriors when he should have led them into Dannu's arms."

The rumble of shock and disgust among the men at such dishonourable deed went unheeded by Parrish. He didn't care if the man had chosen the cowards way out. He was more concerned with the losses incurred among his own men. Scanning the battle site he took a count of those around him. Including two Danebury men who lay on the far side, struck down by arrows, he realized with sadness that he had lost nine men. It seemed he would always hate that number. Before it was possible to gather the names of the fallen, he heard his name called from behind. Looking again to the far side he recognized his holy man, kneeling beside a fallen warrior. The injured man was recognizable to all long before Parrish reached his side. It was Mars. There was a sudden constriction in his throat as he too knelt beside the stricken man.

Mars was his friend. One of the few who had stood by him and befriended him when he had no friends. In the early days. It was Mars who had made for him the great bow that he was so proud to own. But Mars had lost most of the use of one arm during the last big battle his men had fought in. A brave man. A good man. And now he lay in the little shaman's arms, a single arrow sticking starkly out of his chest. It was obvious even to Parrish that the wound was mortal.

Mars coughed and frothy, bright red blood trickled from the corner of his mouth. The holy man looked up at the Chieftain of Danebury as all the rest of the men gathered silently around. Everyone knew what must now be done.

"Dannu calls him." Was all the little man said.

Parrish understood and looked into Mars' eyes. His friend somehow managed the smallest of smiles and nodded slowly. The constriction in the tall man's throat became almost unbearable, making it difficult for him to breath, but he nodded back and held out one hand. The two men's eyes remained locked together. Someone put a battle axe into his open palm and he gripped the shaft so hard his knuckles glowed white. Everyone who watched appreciated that the weapon was Klud's greatly prized, very rare, polished stone axe.

Parrish rose slowly to his feet and raised the deadly weapon above his head. The silence was complete, even the surrounding forest seemed to hold its breath. Mars just offered his tall friend one last smile. A tear trickled from the corner of Parrish's eye and ran unchecked down his cheek. He could not balk now. A good eye and a steady hand would be his last gift to Mars. To make it swift and clean. With an acknowledging nod he swung the axe, and killed his friend.

"It had to be." The holy man's words were cold comfort and Parrish ignored them, staring for a moment at the now bloodied weapon in his fist, then hurled it with all his might far off into the trees. Klud stepped up beside his friend, unconcerned with the loss of his treasured possession. He laid a hand on his arm.

"Come, my Chieftain. Let us go home now."

14

As the men of Danebury accompanied their Chieftain and his friend and fellow warrior Klud on the final leg of their astounding round trip, there was much cheery chatter from among the group. The excited talk was of their victory, trophies gained and the safe return to them of their leader. It was also a great source of pride to them that through the grace of Dannu they had been on hand at the vital moment to save him from certain death. And there too at the vital moment to have the honour of witnessing the great courage that Parrish and Klud had displayed. Even as the group had arrived the two were already running towards glory and death, fearless and brave as they rushed towards Dannu's waiting arms. But she did not let them die and so their Chieftain still walked among them. It was a great honour to be led by such a man.

The only men who were not full of themselves were Parrish and Klud. Both held silent council with their own thoughts. Klud wrestled with his inner turmoil while Parrish just looked about at his warriors, men he had great affection for and was justly proud of, wondering if they at all understood how all the recent deaths were solely down to him. How many more must yet die because he had once broken his word and lost his honour?

At that moment the holy man fell in alongside the tall man, walking quickly to keep up with the bigger man's long strides. He never spoke but just waited. There would be a question, he knew.

Parrish resisted for a while but had to know. Finally, he looked down at the little shaman, gave a small, wry smile and spoke.

"How did you know where we were?"

"Dannu." was the brief reply. Parrish's eyebrows shot up. "Because she smiles on you." The little man added.

"Huh?"

The holy man sighed. Did the tall one still not believe? The proof was overwhelming to all and still he could not see that he was Dannu's man. Friend of the earth and instrument of the Earth Goddess, for her to wield when she saw fit or necessary. Once more it apparently needed to be explained to the Chieftain what he must already know deep in his heart.

"No sooner had I arrived at the great temple of Dannu then I was ordered to return at once to Dane-bre."

The shaman paused for a moment, recalling the urgency of the gathering in the great shrine house of the holy ones. All the elders were there as Dannu drew them together then spoke, and the Danebury shaman found himself almost unwittingly the centre of attention as she directed her words at him. It was his greatest moment then, to be a focus for the Earth Goddess, and his instructions to gather up all the warriors of Dane-bre and lead them to a place of her choosing had been so powerful, so undeniable. Without so much as a pause even for food or rest, with the prayers and good wishes of the elders to carry him along, he had set off at best pace to return to his home village.

The warriors of course rallied to him without question and as one they set off in what seemed to be totally the wrong direction, going virtually due south into territory that no man had walked before. None that is except Parrish, who periodically travelled south, to return again a few days later with fresh feathers from the sky spirits with which to fletch his long reaching spirit arrows.

And yet even with their fear of the unknown, for who knew what lay in the mysterious south land of the Earth Goddess, the massed men of Dane-bre had followed their holy man. They knew he was being guided by Dannu's hand. And it was true, for the little shaman could hear the faint whispers that crept into his head from he knew not where, telling him the way to go.

As he travelled there was an enormous feeling within him that the land was open to the passage of Parrish's men. Nothing would bar their way, there would be no mishaps and wherever it was they were being led to, they would arrive, *must* arrive, in time.

The holy man looked up at Parrish, wondering for a moment just how powerful this tall stranger might really be.

"There was a gathering in the shrine house of the elders." he continued finally. Parrish nodded. He too had once been in this great house and knew it was a place of strength and power. "Dannu spoke to us and I returned to Dane-bre, gathered up all your warriors and led them to you."

"But how did you know which way?"

"She just led me." The little shaman shrugged. He could not explain quite how he knew the way either but he would always remember the feeling of power and oneness with the land and would be grateful to the Earth Goddess, and her man, for allowing him the brief but magnificent taste of it.

The words were of course totally inadequate as an answer to Parrish's question but he decided not to push it further. He felt it was enough that the holy man believed in his goddess and that the warriors were right there when it had mattered most. The why no longer mattered so much in the end. He nodded his thanks to the little shaman, who took the action as a compliment, and turned his attention once more to his men.

He was pleased to see them all so jovial but could never get used to the way they seemed so easily to shrug off death, even the deaths of people close to them. The warriors themselves only saw the massed men of Dane-bre, triumphant in victory. In contrast, Parrish just saw his warrior group nine men short. It gave him a dreadful sinking feeling in the pit of his stomach to look at the tightly wrapped bodies, being carried on litters by some of the men, soon to be offered up to the sky spirits.

Klud had his own troubling thoughts and even his fellow warriors could not raise his spirits. Tomps walked alongside his much respected friend for a while, unaware of his concerns. The youngster showed Klud his trophy for the umpteenth time, holding the head by its hair in front of the older man's face.

"One more to add to those in my stall." He said gleefully. Once cleaned and displayed, the skull would bring his total to four. Indeed, not a bad tally at all for so young a warrior. "The Chieftain has once again provided the chance to gain many trophies for the whole village." The reverent way he felt about his friend Parrish was clear in the tone of his voice. "He will make Dane-bre the strongest village in the whole of Dannu's land."

It was a boast but one that Klud agreed with. He nodded.

"Yes. And you did well today my young friend. It is a good trophy, well won."

"I did well?!" Tomps gasped, amazed at Klud's unconcerned attitude. "I did nothing compared to you and Parrish. We all saw how you had both emptied your quivers and, with nothing more than the weapons in your hands, ran without fear towards the many warriors of Amaldach-bre. Never have I seen such a brave thing! The story of that will be told around campfires for all time."

Klud uncharacteristically waved the accolade aside. He was usually the first to make good out of his own achievements but he did not consider his stance with Parrish an act of bravery. His loyalty to his Chieftain was total and he would follow him anywhere. To the death if he so wished. It was not a thing Klud really thought about. It was just so.

"Perhaps. But you are the one with the trophy. I am sure that there will be a great celebration in the village when we all return."

"Yes!" exclaimed Tomps, his grim widening even more. "I must talk of this with the others."

He bowed respectfully to Klud, who nodded back, then dashed off back into the crowd.

It was very late in the day when the tired troupe finally returned to Danebury. Never had Parrish been so glad to see his home.

All the women turned out to greet their men and it was a moment of mixed emotions for everyone. The wives could not openly display their feelings at the return of their husbands but how they felt was plain to see in their eyes. Truly the bulk of the downtrodden ladies of Dane-bre were more attached to their husbands than they would normally let on. They were happy to see them. And yet there were some whose husbands did not return and their silent sadness was, for Parrish at least, an anguish to watch. He knew the bereaved families would not suffer as individual units within the village structure because the eldest male naturally took over as family leader, but that did nothing to ease Parrish's guilt at seeing himself as the reason for the poor family's losses.

He immediately declared a night of rest for all in the village with the promise that the following night would be one of celebration and thanks to the Earth Goddess at the safe and triumphant return of the men of Dane-bre.

There were gratifying murmurs from everyone at such a wise

decision. Everyone was looking forward to the coming celebration but although no one would admit the strain they had all been under they were none-the-less glad of the prospect of a good night's rest. Besides, the warriors needed time to ready their fresh trophies and so be able to display them proudly on the walls of their stalls during the festivities. This brought up another matter.

Many of the fighting men were curious as to how their Chieftain would react to the fact that some of his warriors had secured trophies while he himself had none. Would it seem as if this proved themselves greater warriors than him?

They need not have worried for Parrish seemed totally indifferent to this potential insult. Praising those among them who had done so well in the name of Dannu and Dane-bre, he announced that through his warrior's victories he claimed a victory also, even if he had no spoils to show. He knew that *all* had done well and so no one could lose face. The men's admiration for him grew even more. Truly he was a great Chieftain.

Even so, all was not right with Parrish of Dane-bre and the village was well aware of the fact. After wishing his warriors a well earned, peaceful nights rest, he set off towards his own house. His dutiful wife fell in a few steps behind and they walked away up the long slope. No words had been spoken between them and there were many sorrowful glances at their backs as made their way towards the suddenly lonely looking cabin atop the hill.

Juli was more relieved than she could ever express at the safe return of Parrish. She had talked with Klud's wife and the woman's words had sent Juli even deeper into despair. She had felt then almost certain that her husband would be gone from her forever.

Yet he was back and her private joy at his safe return knew no bounds, even if she could not outwardly show it. How she longed to rush to his arms but there was no love left in him now she knew, and so he was cold to her. Her heart was breaking and, with all his acute powers of observation, could he not see?

But all her tall husband did, seemingly oblivious to the poor girl's sufferings, was leave her to cook, ate the food she prepared for him, then slept. The next day he spent deep in sober thought, watching the village from his usual vantage point at the top of the knoll. Not once had he spoken directly to her.

Klud too had not spoken since his return and as the celebration approached, both men were glaring in their silence among the bubbling festivities that were going on around them.

The entire village had now gathered inside the huge shrine hut, each family filling its allotted stall and anticipating a good evening of worship, praise then joyous celebration, followed by feasting and dancing to the throb of the drums. Everything was prepared, but nothing could start until the holy man was ready and there was a delay. A delay because the Chieftain had called the shaman over to his stall just before he was to begin.

"What is it you want?" The holy man's eyebrows shot up in query at this unusual move. It would normally cause great offence to interrupt a holy man but he knew that Parrish would not do so without good reason.

The tall man pulled him closer and nodded across the great hut to where Klud sat sullenly in the back of his stall opposite. It was plain the normally boisterous warrior was not himself.

"My friend is not in good spirits. I would like you to find out why." He looked down at the holy man. "He has done more than well in these past, difficult days and has no cause to feel bad. He is my good friend and so before I have to order him to speak up about his troubles, I would ask that you talk to him. Find out what ails him and let me know if there is anything that I can do."

"As you wish." The shaman nodded tightly and quickly made his way across to Klud's stall.

The Neolithic warrior noticed the man's approach and rose respectfully to his feet. At a beckoning sign he followed the little man and together they walked silently around the hut and disappeared from view behind the huge statue of the Great Goddess into the space behind.

Here was where the holy man had his living quarters. It was strangely quiet and both men squatted on the earth floor in the dimmer light, Klud trying not to look too obviously at all the strange pots, emblems and religious paraphernalia that lay strewn about, stacked in piles or daubed on the wall.

"You are not happy." The words were blunt and to the point. "Whatever troubles you, it would be better if spoken of rather than kept quiet to poison you from the inside."

Klud knew he spoke true and yet it would hurt to say what he felt. But the holy one had spoken and Klud did not know how to lie. He was an honest warrior and his word was his bond. He let out a long sigh before speaking in hushed tones.

"I have denied Dannu." he said quietly.

"What!?" exploded the shaman before pursing his lips shut and lapsing into a thoughtful silence. This could not be. He knew each and every person of Dane-bre and Klud was a true and faithful warrior of the Earth Goddess. One of the best. Something very strange must have happened out there in the wild land to make such a man denounce his firmest beliefs.

"Tell me what has happened." he said softly, and Klud, with a pained look on his face, relayed to him how when he and Parrish were all but lost, left to their fate, he had denied the Earth Goddess. How he had instead allied himself forever with his friend and Chieftain before they ran together towards certain death. But they had not died and now he could not console himself over his moment of doubt of the righteousness of Dannu. He had rejected her in his moment of need and now felt sure that she would no longer accept his worship of her. She would not believe him and he knew he was not worthy. He finished by flatly stating that he knew there was no place for him here at the village shrine hut and was sure there would now be no place for him in the great shrine house of the Earth Goddess after his death.

The holy man understood his fears well enough but could not understand how the man doubted Dannu's faith in such a brave warrior.

"Klud." he said firmly. "You need not worry. I can see that the Earth Goddess is as strong with you now as before, if not stronger. I will not deny that you were wrong to doubt her in your moment of death, but I have yet to meet any man who did not when his time was at hand. After all, no mortal has ever yet returned from Dannu's arms to say how good the next life is. This is not to say that it is not so but to us, the living, death is a great leap into a strange new land. I do not doubt that when my time comes, I too shall falter before taking that final step."

"You?" gasped Klud.

"Yes. And even if you did deny Dannu for that one moment, did you not stand there beside her man and match him step for step towards her waiting arms? If she in turn had doubted you, do you think she would have saved you as well as Parrish? I was there and saw also. So many arrows flew that for you both to have lived needed the greatest attention from Dannu. You must know that you are alive because of her. Because of her and your loyal stand with her man." It was a statement rather than a question. He nodded solemnly as he too suddenly understood the truth. "To stand by him *is* to stand with her."

The holy man slowly folded his arms across his chest, magnanimous in the monumental speech he had just made. Klud was simply astounded. Apart from Parrish's own lips, he had never heard such great words. He looked at the shaman, knowing how close all the holy ones were to Dannu and well aware of how this man in particular had spoken with Dannu and been guided by her to their rescue. His words were undeniably true and he believed them utterly. Prophetic words that Klud would never forget.

To stand by Parrish was to stand with Dannu.

The warrior rose slowly to his feet, took a deep, satisfying breath then broke into a wide grin.

"You are a great man." He said with real feeling. "And Dannu chooses her servants well. I thank you for your wise words and go now to give thanks to Dannu too." He bowed deeply to the holy man, a gesture which surprised the shaman but he took graciously, then left the shadowy alcove and returned to his stall, to the others of the village apparently restored as if by magic to the laughing, boisterous Klud that everyone knew. As the little holy man also appeared, making his way towards the Chieftains stall, there were more than a few puzzled but respectful glances in his direction.

"Well done." Parrish had been quick to notice the immediate change in his friend. "What ailed him?"

The holy man dismissed the whole episode with a simple wave of his hand. A lesser man might have grasped the chance to make personal glory of the achievement but the shaman was above that. Standing next to a man who he considered to be great, he showed his own greatness.

"It was a simple matter between Klud and Dannu." was the modest reply. "We spoke together and it will not trouble him again."

Parrish accepted the rather bland answer. He knew there was more to it than was being let on, but if it was a problem of religion then the holy man was the best person to sort it out. He pressed the subject no further.

"I still say you did well and thank you for it."

The shaman simply nodded at the gratitude then walked out and stood before the statue of the Earth Goddess. Silence fell as he readied himself to start the evening's festivities with heartfelt prayers to Dannu.

15

The celebrations were of course a great success. The holy man's rhetoric made Danebury's warriors seem all conquering and the proud men danced and stamped long into the night, those with new trophies ignoring their sore necks where freshly scored tattooed circles denoted their courage. Women and children clapped along to the thumping rhythm and everyone had a full belly. Yes, it was a good night.

The only surprise of the evening, which set tongues wagging for a long time after, was an announcement by the Chieftain. Surprise that he even needed to tell anyone of his intentions, because he was Chieftain and could do as he wished, and surprise at the nature of the announcement.

Parrish on the other hand felt that as his village had been instrumental in the recent events, they must be involved in the final acts of those events.

"I am going on another trip." He declared after calling the gathering to silence. There were many eyebrows raised in both surprise and curiosity. "And I will take some warriors with me. I am to return to Amaldach-bre!"

There were a few gasps and the odd scoff. No one would ask him why he would do this but Parrish knew they were curious and he wanted to explain.

"I think the village there now holds nothing but women and children. It is true that we have beaten their warriors in battle, in an honourable fight, but I am not a killer of women and children." The faces around him showed confusion now.

They did not understand his twentieth century ideals. What happened to a group of people several days walk away surely had nothing to do with the people of Dane-bre?

But Parrish had other ideas.

"If we just leave them they will surely die, without their warriors to protect and provide for them." The looks on the faces of his own warriors said, so what? "So I am going back to Amaldach-bre to gather up the people there."

This time the curiosity of those gathered around him could not be contained. The shaman was their spokesman and he voiced their one thought.

"And what will you do with these people Parrish?" He was not in the least sceptical in his tone, just genuinely curious. There was no need to state the obvious fact that Danebury could not support many more than already lived inside its wall.

"I am glad you ask." said Parrish, fixing the little man with a small, knowing smile. "Because I am sure that you will want to come on this journey too. I am going to gather up all the people and take them to the great temple of Dannu."

There were immediate murmurings from the crowd and, from out of the corner of his eye, he noticed a few discreet nods of agreement from the women.

They understood his carefully concealed appreciation of the womenfolk of the village and instantly felt his decision was the right thing to do for the poor widows of the decimated village.

"I believe you have work to do there." he added, still addressing the shaman. "And it is my opinion that the women of Amaldach-bre could live in the great village and serve Dannu's chosen ones. Better that than to die at the hands of the first raiding party that comes along."

It was a bit more complicated than that. There were other things to consider.

He would naturally permit any of his men to take an extra wife from among the women of Amaldach-bre, if they so chose, and he had no idea if there would be any opposition to his plan from the holy men of Windmill Hill, the huge causewayed camp above the great temple. But he had every intention of doing his utmost to see that no more died than had to because of his actions.

There were a few moments of silence while the holy man

considered the Chieftains words. It was another unexpected, unprecedented even, act from the Chieftain of Dane-bre but then, that was one of his great strengths. And yet somehow the idea struck the right chord even in the Neolithic attitude filled mind of the little shaman. There was indeed something to be said for the tall man's strange ways.

Having recently returned from the great temple, at his village's time of crisis, he knew that helping hands were always needed back there. The village of the chosen ones would be strengthened by the extra women who would add support to the warriors there as well as the holy men. And it was true, as Parrish had said, that he himself had unfinished work there concerning his young heir. The training of his successor had barely begun and it was very necessary for the apprentices own holy man to be on hand at the start of his path to enlightenment, to ensure that in all the wonders that he might learn, he did not lose sight of the individual needs of his own village among the great scheme of things. The shaman also wondered just what exactly the reaction of the holy ones might be to Parrish's arrival. There were to be interesting times ahead for the religious men of Dannu's land. Of course the little shaman would go with his Chieftain.

"I would be honoured to go with you to Amaldach-bre." he said finally. "It will be something to see indeed." He did not add that it would also be interesting to see if the people there would bow readily to his wishes. Would a whole clan leave their village and their homes, forever, on the word of a complete stranger?

Parrish nodded his approval.

"We leave the day after tomorrow." he pronounced to everyone loudly, then strode through the gathered people, who parted bowing before him, and left the great hut without a backward glance, leaving the massed people of Danebury in a stunned silence. And Juli stranded all alone in the suddenly deserted Chieftains stall.

The journey, one that had originally taken Parrish alone only twenty hours to travel, this time took the Chieftain and his warrior band two and a half days to complete.

The group was more or less the same one that had set off with him that fateful day to go and prepare his tomb although, because there might, if anything, be more need for fighting than building, he this time allowed Tomps to accompany him. His diminutive wife

Karin naturally followed after her husband. For a moment Parrish wondered if the fact that she was originally from another village might be beneficial. Perhaps a few favourable words from her might help the women of Amaldach-bre adjust to a new environment? He quickly dismissed the thought, knowing that a Chieftain could not be seen to ask a mere woman for assistance. To his warrior's females had their place. To carry for and feed their men.

Among these women, as was expected of her and her rightful place, was the Chieftain's wife. Parrish rather she hadn't come along, not wishing to put her through the extra agonies of having to remain so close for such a length of time to the man he knew she now despised. This would include the extra distance to and back home from Dannu's temple at Hambledon Hill.

Juli just continued to carry out the tasks of a dutiful wife, tending to her husband's needs but keeping her own council, barely speaking at all during the entire journey. The other women rallied around her but as the girl's problem was one that no Neolithic woman had ever encountered before, all they could do was try to offer her comfort.

Now they all stood looking at the main gate of Amaldach-bre, just a long arrow shot away from them. There were still wisps of campfire smoke rising from inside the hillfort but the lack of men along the parapet was almost glaring in its absence.

The first obstacle to Parrish's plan was to gain entry to the village.

He nocked one of his black fletched arrows to his great bow, drew and launched the slender missile towards the main gate. It struck with a hard thud and stuck quivering in the timber frontage. He could see, even from the distance, that it grabbed the immediate attention of those inside the camp.

After giving them a few minutes to think about it he handed all his weapons to Klud then slowly approached the gate, arms held away from his sides to show he was unarmed. Although his intentions towards the people of Amaldach-bre were purely honourable, Parrish knew that it would not do to show weakness and ask or plead with them to open the gate. He was a Chieftain and demanded respect. A firm line was needed.

"Open the gates to me or I will order my warriors to attack!" he barked loudly. There was no immediately noticeable response. "Do not try my patience." he shouted. "Talking is surely better than death."

Only a few moments after the blatant threat the huge gate began to swing slowly open. As it swung wide it was immediately apparent that several women were needed to help pull it back. There weren't even enough men left to open the front door!

An old man ambled out of the entrance, paused momentarily then moved forward with the clear intention of having a parlay with him. Even so, the warriors of Danebury rushed forward in defence of their Chieftain. He stopped them with a raised hand and they all gathered behind him, everyone watching the old man's approach.

Parrish was actually expecting the villages representative to be its holy man and was a bit disappointed, wondering just how much clout this old one had in his village. Perhaps he was the elder statesman of Amaldach-bre? All eyes watched the man closely as he drew near.

Perhaps it was inaccurate, even insulting, to call him an old man.

Although he was beaten and bowed by many years of hard toil and battle, with a wrinkled, weather beaten brow and gnarled hands, the man was in reality only a little over thirty five years old. The slightly fading tattoo's he wore said that he was once a brave fighter and could command at least some measure of respect. He approached boldly enough but when their eyes met the fear was there. He expected to be cut down any second. As Chieftain, Parrish naturally had right of lead.

"A wise choice old man. Do you know who I am?"

"You are Parrish of Dane-bre, and these are some of your warriors." The old man briefly eyed the twenty men just a few paces back, all their eyes still locked onto him. "It was you and the one called Klud that all our warriors set off after to kill."

"Do not wait any more for your men to return." Parrish gave him the bad news straight. There was no easy way to say what needed to be said. "Dannu has them now."

The impact of the words physically shocked the man and he swayed as if he had been struck. Although it was not done to directly question a Chieftain the words still came out.

"How ... how many?"

"All."

The old man shook his head, at first Parrish thought in defiance.

"Not all. Our Chieftain and two of his men returned some days ago."

"Huh?" Now it was Parrish's' turn to be shocked. "Are they still here?"

"No. They gathered fresh supplies and quickly left again."

"Did he say what had happened to the rest of his warriors?"

The old man simply shook his head.

"Well, believe me when I say this, all the other warriors of Amaldach-bre have gone into the arms of the Earth Goddess. And now it seems that your Chieftain has gone completely mad, fled like a coward and left the remains of his village to the will of Dannu."

The old man believed Parrish's words all right. He was well known as a man who spoke strange, but true. Besides, the aged warrior had looked into the tall one's eyes and knew instinctively that there was no lie there. In simple acknowledgment the breath sighed out of him, his shoulders sagged and a look of utter defeat swept over his face.

Parrish stepped up and laid a compassionate hand on the Neolithic man's shoulder.

"Let us go inside and talk." He spoke softly. "Perhaps we can find a way out of this trouble."

What else was there to be done? The old man nodded slowly without looking up then turned and led the way back into Amaldach-bre, followed closely by the tall Chieftain and his men.

Parrish cast a critical eye around the village as the warrior band walked through on their way to the central shrine hut. It seemed so alien to witness a village with no men folk at all. Alive yet somehow dead. His men immediately spread out, looking for any useful equipment and weapons to take back home. This was not looting as far as they were concerned, but part of the battle. To the victors went the spoils. Even so, they were under orders not to harm any of the women of the village.

When Parrish entered the shrine hut, Klud as ever at his side, he was confronted by a deputation that had been gathered to meet him. They stood in a tight group before the central fire. Beyond them, at the rear of the hut, the bulbous statue of the Earth Goddess rose above them, looking somehow almost foreboding in the half light. At the head of the group was the holy man of Amaldach-bre, his face still bruised by Parrish's assault.

Including him and the old man who had led in, they numbered only five.

"Is this all?" asked Parrish, rather shocked by the total absence of any fighting men. In reply all the men just bowed deeply.

"Then there will be no talks." He said firmly. "Go and gather all the people of the village together. I wish to speak to them and tell them all what I have decided to do."

There was instant trepidation on the faces before him but none dare refuse and they all bowed again then hurried past to do his bidding.

Shaking his head Parrish turned to Klud, the pair now alone in the great hut.

"Just a few old men. The village could not protect itself against even the smallest raiding party."

Klud nodded in agreement.

"So it seems. Your victory against the village of Amaldach-bre is complete."

Parrish just scoffed at that and left the hut quickly, leaving Klud to realize that he was now all alone in the shrine hut with just the statue of the Earth Goddess towering over him. Eyeing the tall, rounded sculpture for a moment, the silence seemed to descend like a smothering blanket. Feeling suddenly and unexplainably intimidated, he spun on his heel and hurried out to join Parrish in the warm sunshine.

The victorious Chieftain of Dane-bre sat cross-legged on the ground in front of the entrance to the great hut, watching in silence as the entire remaining population of Amaldach-bre was rounded up by his men and gathered before him. Women of all ages, a few young teenage boys and small children clinging to their mother's skirts were all that now remained of a recently thriving village. A once proud people, they were now being herded like sheep by the seated man's warriors and shuffled meekly along, only those pitifully few old men showing token resistance. They placed themselves at the head of the group between Parrish and their women, a brave but totally futile gesture of protection. At the head of the crowd, now at last taking his place as the leader of his remaining flock, stood the holy man of Amaldach-bre, defiantly dressed in his full religious regalia. If it hadn't been such a serious situation Parrish might have allowed himself a smile. He was warming to the man despite the barely concealed anger on the face still marked by his fist.

At that moment Klud approached and Parrish rose effortlessly to his feet, listening in silence as the Neolithic man pronounced all the huts inside the fort checked and that every person who lived here now stood before him. The warriors of Danebury were well positioned around the edges of the crowd to deter any foolhardy attempts at dashing off, containing the people simply with their frightening presence. Parrish nodded in satisfaction and Klud took up his customary position by his Chieftains right hand.

The Danebury women stood in a cluster off to one side, watching in silence. They knew what the Chieftain was about to propose and all hoped that things would go as he wished. If only the women of Amaldach-bre knew how the tall one understood the ways of Dannu's women, they would not hesitate to go with him.

Juli watched how every single face was captured and held by the presence of her husband. Most were plainly frightened, some intimidated and a few curious, but all without exception were drawn to him. She could feel his power and her chest burned hot with the pride she felt for him. Even if he no longer loved her, she knew she would still worship him until the day she died.

There were a few long, drawn out moments of tense silence, during which the Chieftains own holy man emerged from the great hut and joined the group, standing on Parrish's left. The little shaman had been rummaging through the religious goods behind the statue inside. Neither was this looting. His intention was to take whatever he felt important back to the great temple and the village of the chosen ones.

Seeing this show of unity from the men of Danebury the Hambledon Hill holy man stepped forward and spoke loudly and defiantly.

"Does Dannu agree with this attack?" he snarled the words at his opposite number, not daring to ask an aggressive question directly to a Chieftain but still determined to get his message across. "Will she agree to the slaughter of her women?"

Parrish raised his hand for silence and shot the man a withering stare.

"There will be no slaughter." he barked. "You can live or die as you please. I have come here simply to give you the choice."

The holy man's expression changed from anger to confusion. Parrish continued, speaking loudly and slowly so all could hear and understand.

"Know now that apart from your mad Chieftain, who has deserted you in your moment of greatest need, all the other warriors of Amaldach-bre fought against me and my warriors with great courage and honour, but they will never again return to their village. Even as we speak they travel into Dannu's arms." He felt it prudent not to mention that they would never enter the great spiritual shrine house of the Earth Goddess because their bodies were not whole, their heads now being displayed as trophies on the walls of his own warriors stalls. This 'small' omission went unnoticed as many of the women gasped, shocked at the enormity of his bold statement. He forged on, not allowing them time to dwell on the bad news.

"You are now an unprotected village." He did not feel the need either to point out the implications of this, the simple presence of his own warriors was proof enough. "The choice then is yours. Come with me on my terms or stay here and await certain death."

The women of course had no say and it fell to the holy man, temporary leader, to speak for his people. He glanced at the Danebury shaman who gave him a brief nod of encouragement. The man was not convinced but knew the choice was no choice. Even so, he was a proud man and so there was a lengthy silence before he finally bowed to the inevitable and asked quietly.

"What are your terms?"

Parrish gave a barely discernible sigh of relief and once more addressed the crowd.

"I have not come to kill you. Come with me and I will lead you to the great temple of the Earth Goddess, where you can live on and serve the chosen ones in their large village beyond the stones." He doubted very few had ever seen beyond the temple itself. "Your lives will still have purpose. To serve Dannu is a great honour. Is this not better than death?" To his surprise there was no immediate reaction, either for or against. "My warriors will give you protection on the walk there. I promise you safe passage. If a warrior of mine wishes to take one of you for another wife I will allow it. These women will then return with their new husbands and become a part of my village. The rest will live to serve the holy ones. Do you agree?"

After a few moments the Amaldach-bre holy man stepped forward, mouth open to speak. Parrish waved him silent, much to the man's annoyance, and eyed the crowd, scanning the astonished faces.

"I ask you all now. Do you agree to my terms?"

The massed women were at first just amazed by the simple fact of being addressed directly by a Chieftain, let alone being given the opportunity to voice their own opinion by being given a choice. There was much uncomfortable shuffling of feet and indistinct mumbles.

Parrish knew that they would not easily if at all be able to come to a decision, never having been asked to do so before. They would be more concerned with pleasing the surrounding men folk and honouring their village rather than putting their own interests first. But he desperately wanted to do the right thing by them and so decided to help them along the right road with a little Neolithic psychology, more properly called intimidation.

"WELL?!" he barked sharply, appearing to be impatient and folding his arms aggressively across his chest. Muttered words of agreement and a sea of quickly nodding heads was the instant reply. He stifled a grin.

"Good! Gather up whatever goods you would carry with you on the journey. At first light tomorrow we leave the village of Amaldachbre forever."

It was a very final statement.

With an apparently dismissive wave of his hand he signalled the crowd to go, spun on his heel and went back inside the shrine hut, his back hiding the satisfied look on his face. Behind him the women, old men and village holy man just stood, slack jawed and with looks of amazement on their faces.

16

The next morning, bright and early, the crowd gathered once again before the entrance to the great hut. All the women were now laden down with their possessions and any foodstuffs they would need for the journey ahead. Most of the Danebury warriors also carried an extra item or two, their spoils of war.

When Parrish at last emerged to see all the women gathered there before him, his first reaction was a smile. But then, seeing all the timid faces and the tiny female bodies, their vulnerability and dependence on their now lost warriors, he suddenly wanted to gather them too him in protection. It made him remember just how much he missed holding Juli. The thought pained him and he tried to push it aside, concentrating on the task ahead, unaware of his mouth setting into a grim line.

Every face was again turned to him and there seemed to be an air of expectancy. Puzzled, he turned to Klud, eyebrows raised in question. His friend leaned in close and whispered.

"They are waiting for your words Parrish." he explained. "At a time such as this, a Chieftain would speak to the people."

Parrish nodded in sudden realization. An announcement or proclamation of some sort was in order. Yes, he recalled, looking back at past events within his own village. Whenever something important, let alone anything as monumental as a village evacuation was about to happen, Chieftain Coran would normally have made a speech. But he had been a great man who spoke great words. What on earth could Parrish say to impress and motivate those before him now?

He scanned the faces, both his own warriors and the cluster of women, for a few moments then drew himself up to full height.

"Women of Amaldach-bre." He said loudly. "You are of Amaldach-bre no more. We set off now for the great temple of Dannu and your new home. On the journey there do not try to run off and escape from my warriors. It would be no escape. Know this. My men will not chase after you and bring you back. They are there to protect you, not to hunt you down. If you run you will be left to your fate. You will be all alone in Dannu's land with her wilderness, her animals and perhaps even hunting parties." He did not need to elaborate any further on the folly of such an action.

"We go now, so take a last look at your old village." As if to order heads swivelled and scanned the emptiness of the work areas, the deserted found houses and their cold, extinguished fires. "Do not remember this place as a bad village. Just a village with a bad Chieftain." He let that sink in for a few moments. "And now we shall leave."

People picked up their various bundles, slung packs on their backs and gathered their children to them. Klud stepped up close beside his tall friend.

"Great words my Chieftain." he said reverently.

To his surprise Parrish let out a laugh, clapped him on the back in appreciation of the complement and, shaking his head in private amusement, led off towards the main gate.

Parrish allowed himself another of his rare, wry smiles as he watched the predominantly female crowd ahead of him, making its way across the green and fertile landscape. It seemed to him that in recent times all he appeared to do was travel back and forth across the land. Way back in his past, or was it his future, he recalled having that simple yet noble wish for a family and a quiet life. But it was by now apparent that he was destined to live anything but that.

As the exodus from Amaldach-bre progressed and time began to string out like the miles between the travellers and their departure point, he could see the women gradually becoming a little more at ease with their escort of foreign warriors.

There was no ill will toward them they now realized. If anything, the men of Danebury seemed almost indifferent to their fears. They were simply carrying out the wishes of their Chieftain. Also, his earlier offer of a 'free' wife to any warrior who wanted was originally very tempting but, after some more serious consideration, it became obvious that another addition to a family group meant extra clothing, food, living space and responsibility. Only those men with a genuine shortage of womenfolk in his individual family group still seriously considered the offer after the first day's travel.

By the time the group settled for its second night out under the stars the men, who were greatly outnumbered by women, were being almost pampered by the attention given to their needs by the women.

With camp and sentries established, the warriors barely needed to lift a finger to obtain whatever they needed. An extra covering, water, food or even sex if they so desired it because by this second day the Amaldach-bre women had come to understand their own position after considering more what lay ahead for them all.

Living and working in the village of the holy ones would of course be an honour, although it was unknown as to how they would be received there, assuming they would be accepted and allowed to stay there at all. The ladies dare not ask any of the men about this and so it remained a great question mark above them.

A more certain future seemed to lay with their warrior escort. The Danebury women who had accompanied their men were, in total contrast to the warriors, quite happy to mix with and speak to their own kind and were full of praise for their village and its strange Chieftain. Dane-bre appeared to be a happy, safe and prosperous place. And so it was that the misplaced women of Amaldach-bre soon grasped the idea that life in Dane-bre might be a better alternative to the fast approaching unknown fate awaiting them all at the temple of the Earth Goddess. And that was why they began to take more and more interest in the warriors escorting them, being ever more helpful and attentive to any needs they might have.

Parrish seemed to be the only man expecting this, the rest unprepared for this strange turn of events. He watched it all from his lofty position as Chieftain, knowing that no female would dare approach him directly. The only woman to attend him was his own wife, whom he seemed to be coldly indifferent to. This attitude toward her actually put off all thoughts from the other ladies of currying any favour with the tall man.

The Chieftain just watched in silent amusement as individual Amaldach-bre women attempted to attach themselves to their 'chosen' warrior, sometimes with the gratitude of his wife who was glad of the extra help with the carrying and chores, but in other instances met by what verged on open hostility against her by the warriors legitimate wife, who saw the outsider as attempting to invade her private territory.

Most of the men could not care less, happy of the extra attention but already, as Parrish had correctly deduced, decided for themselves whether or not they needed an extra wife. He was sure those still interested would approach him for permission to add to their 'harem' at the end of the walk, if indeed any had chosen.

But that did in no way dissuade the women of Amaldach-bre from their advances.

Parrish could not help but smile secretly as he watched in particular how several women at once were trying to ingratiate themselves with young Tomps. The lad couldn't believe his good fortune. Never had he been so popular! It had not yet occurred to him that he was considered more than a good catch for any lowly woman. It was plain to all of them that not only was Tomps blatantly young and virile, he also proudly bore the tattoos of a brave and undoubtedly accomplished battle warrior. So many trophies for one so young. It soon became known too that not only was he the youngest warrior of his village to have his own stall in Dane-bre's shrine hut, he also seemed to have the private ear of the Chieftain, a rare achievement for any warrior. But most significant of all to the women of Amaldach-bre was the discovery that he only had one wife and she too was an outsider!

As the group crossed the last of the big rivers and travelled up onto Salisbury Plain, a route which Parrish had no choice in using because to circumvent the open land would add perhaps five more days to the trip, he spread his scouts further afield to lessen the risk of any surprise attacks and help alleviate a nagging feeling he had in the back of his mind. But apart from commanding his warriors to the best advantage he really had little else to do other than lead and to watch the social juggling going on around him.

It was clear, to him at least, that Karin was suffering badly under the onslaught of several Amaldach-bre women, all intent on wrestling her young husbands affections from her, while she could do little more than look on in silent dismay. Their many hands could have food prepared, clothing repaired, water to hand and equipment carried for the man long before she could, it being physically impossible for her to do so many tasks at once. And all the girl could do was suffer in silence, unable to complain to her husband who was enjoying all the attention or fight off the combined assaults of several women at once.

Yet as Chieftain of Dane-bre it was Parrish's' job, and his great honour, to look after the welfare of his people, either collectively or individually.

He caught up with Karin later that day as she and several other women were vying for the best watering point at a tiny rivulet discovered along the route.

At his approach all the women bowed deeply, almost cowering with respect. He gruffly ordered them all away and they scuttled off clutching their still empty skin water bags to their chests.

"Not you." he barked, pointing at Karin. She froze, wondering what she had done to warrant her Chieftains personal attention, and dreading what might happen next. The others now left in even greater haste, shooting dubious rearward glances in the pairs direction as they went.

Then the two were alone, the main group and its warrior guard moving on, away in the mid distance. Standing over six feet tall in his boots, Parrish towered over the tiny Neolithic girl who in comparison was slightly less than five foot in height, and she stood in trembling silence, head bowed.

He sat down cross legged on the ground, immediately reversing the height advantage, and bade the girl to look at him. Her head came cautiously up and their eyes met. He smiled.

"I have noticed your trouble with the women of Amaldach-bre and their interest in Tomps."

Karin's eyes widened in surprise. It was true then. He really did see everything with that piercing gaze of his. Parrish nodded at that moment as if he could somehow read her mind.

"What are your thoughts on this?" he asked.

She knew she could not deny the great man his answer and in all honesty she was glad to have the chance to unburden her worries on someone. She had never imagined though that that someone would turn out to be her own Chieftain! Surely he need not bother himself with the petty problems of one woman. And one not born of Dane-bre either. Yet it was true that he had once before offered out the hand of friendship to her. She had not grasped it firmly, partly in fear but mostly out of her respect for the man, not wishing to damage his standing among those of his village. He would lose face if he were seen to mix openly with mere women and as Chieftain that could not be permitted. But now, by his own design, they were alone, a situation that she might take advantage of. She sighed deeply and her hands opened in a gesture of futility.

"I do not know what I can do, my Chieftain. They are so many. It seems my husband no longer needs me."

"That is not so." Parrish gave her what he hoped was an encouraging smile. "He is just blinded by their efforts to please him. But I know Tomps. He is my friend and although he is still young he is fast learning the ways and wisdom of the warrior. You must not give up in your struggle for him. Help him whenever you can, for you will still be there when the others have gone. But there is one thing you must *not* do." Karin's eyebrows shot up in question, her full attention locked on the man and his words. "You must not let them into his bed."

He recalled an old saying regularly heard among his old Army mates, as true now as it was then. Blunt and to the point. 'A stiff prick has no conscience'.

"In that place you must keep them out, if you want to keep your position with him. Fight them if you must. Know this too. In an open contest, if I am asked to settle the problem, I will favour you rather than them because you are a part of the village of Dane-bre. You would have my support then but otherwise there is nothing else I can do without being seen to take over and that would show to one and all that Tomps cannot manage his own affairs. This would shame him in the eyes of the other men. I will not do that but, and I say this just to you alone, if at any time he chooses to ask my advice on the subject, as one man to another, I will try to make him see things in your favour. OK?"

It was more than she could have ever hoped for. Before this moment she had not believed the tall tales spoken by the other Dane-bre women about Dannu's man. But now she knew they were true. He really did care for the women of his village, a totally unprecedented thing. The worry seemed to lift almost magically from her shoulders and a fresh fire rose in her clear eyes.

That's better, thought Parrish, spotting the immediate change.

"Thank you, my Chieftain." she said gratefully. "You are indeed wise. I will do my very best not to disappoint you or the proud name of the village of Dane-bre."

"I could ask no more than that." he replied somewhat magnanimously, rising swiftly to his feet. "Stay close to your man, support him and trust in his judgment. What little I can do without offending him I will indeed do. Now come and I will walk you back to the others."

He turned and set off in the direction of the disappearing crowd, well pleased with the way his little pow-wow had gone. This rather self satisfying glow was immediately dimmed when he became aware that rather than join him and talk with him while they walked, as Juli often did, Karin did the dutiful, female thing and fell silently and respectfully in a few paces behind.

Another and more sinister thing, that Parrish was also gradually becoming more aware of, was confirmed to him that very evening.

He was at the time slightly to one side of the main group, ambling along at their pace, when he gradually slowed his speed then stopped all together, seeming to the casual observer almost as if he had frozen in mid stride. Those of Dane-bre knew the signs though. Their tall Chieftain had once again become one with the earth. Dannu's man was talking with his mistress, joined together with her through the land itself.

After a few moments Klud appeared at his side, as if in answer to a silent call, and together the pair stood side by side in silence for several long minutes, gazing out over the untamed landscape.

"We are being followed. Watched." Klud at last spoke. "I feel it."

"Yes." agreed Parrish and the men once again lapsed into silence, not so much straining their eyes or ears across the land as much as trying to somehow *feel* the nearness or direction of the unknown, watching eyes.

"They are few or we would have already been attacked." Klud was just as sure of his second statement.

"You speak wisely." acknowledged Parrish. "But they may try a raid if the group is allowed to spread. Or perhaps after dark. Make sure the men keep a keen watch this night." The last part of his statement was really unnecessary but he had no intention of taking any stupid chances or exposing those in his charge to needless risks.

"It will be done." Klud nodded and moved away towards the watching crowd. Not once had the two men looked at each other, so in tune were their minds. Each so very different and yet still the same.

17

The walking party travelled on northwards, leaving the open land behind them as they came down off the Plain and threaded their way into the much more heavily wooded valley that would in later times become known as the Vale of Pewsey. There they all spent one more night, ahead of the final push towards their ultimate destination. Parrish thought that everyone would benefit from the rest, enabling them all to arrive at the Gathering Point the next morning fresh and perhaps more receptive to any events that might then take place.

And all through this time the mysterious, shadowing presence was occasionally felt but never once materialized into a more solid threat. The Chieftain, his right hand man and several of the more alert and astute warriors were aware of the unknown threat, the others of the party just following their tall leaders instructions and directions, putting their faith in the righteousness of his actions.

Drawing slowly but ever nearer to the Great Temple, both the holy men in the party now began to prepare their people spiritually for this unscheduled visit to the focal point of all their worship. They occupied their time by passing constantly among the female throng, raising their awareness and making them conscious of their humility before Dannu. This task needed to be done before the imminent arrival at the Gathering Point that nestled in the great bend in the river. It was from here, if the women were to be accepted at all, that they would all walk with pride along the stone lined avenue that led to the Great Temple itself.

Parrish watched the two shaman working together, both in harmony now, any previous differences between them forgotten as they rallied in their shared alliance to a higher order. In a curious way Parrish himself was also looking forward to the meeting ahead. His memories of the great stone circle of Avebury, the causewayed camp above it and the village of holy men who lived there were very vivid and, for the most part, happy. He had learned much when last there and perhaps another chance to talk with the great one, the old man who seemed to know so much, might even arise. Yes, Parrish was in his own way quietly warming to the prospect of at last finishing this journey, seeing the reactions of those at Avebury, and perhaps finally putting an end to this dark chapter in his life. He knew things could never be the same again but at least some good would have come from this whole tragic, sordid affair. Considering just how he had first come to be here in prehistoric southern England, it was somewhat ironic that he now dearly wished he could turn back time. If only he could get a second chance to alter the past and prevent the moment when the whole thing went dreadfully wrong, and stop the terrible events that took place after his meeting with Tanis. Or at least he could have been there when it mattered and done the right thing by his poor wife.

Juli, still mournfully silent and quietly unobtrusive as a wife should be yet still never very far from her husband in case he might suddenly need her, also felt the pangs of remembered joys as she too looked back to her last visit to the Great Temple.

Parrish still had much to learn then and yet his acknowledgment as an equal by an unknown Chieftain, his ignorance and arrogance towards the holy men, the incident at the stone circle on midsummer's morn and that mysterious, never talked about meeting he had had with the great ones of the temple were all still fresh in her mind. The meeting in particular held a special significance. No one could remember such a thing ever taking place before and the event was the talk of all the tribes who had come together at the Gathering Point. She had been so proud of him then. She still was now, although she dare not say so or show it. It hurt so much to know he did not now care for her. Even so, her bond to him was still true and she would not dishonour him, especially at the temple. He was still her husband and she knew she would serve him to the best of her ability now, tomorrow and until the day she died. Juli cast one more careful, discrete look at his strong features in the vain hope of

one small return glimmer of warmth.
Nothing.

Parrish lead the way up over the long ridge that marked the northern edge of the Vale of Pewsey and on to the river crossing where the Kennet was wide and shallow. Only now did he call in his lookouts that had kept constant vigil on either flank. Now he felt confident that there would be no attacks, not this close to the temple of Dannu. This river was the same one that swept around the southernmost aspect of the Gathering Point, no further than three or four miles away downstream. He waited patiently as everyone else forded across then let the holy men take the lead, as was their right, and they all set off through the last stretch of woodland, keeping the river close on their left.

The anticipation could be felt by everyone now. Irrespective of the eventual outcome of their arrival, the approach to the central worshipping point of all the southern lands still demanded respect and reverence. The annual bartering that took place there after the touching of the stone ceremony at midsummer always brought out the best in Dannu's people. It was an event always looked forward to by one and all.

This time it would be different but the place was still the same. Holy ones would surely be there and Dannu would of course be very close at hand. All those now journeying under the protection of the tall man were well aware of his closeness to the Earth Goddess and they all wondered what, if anything, might happen upon his arrival? There was most certain to be interesting times ahead.

Finally, with a sigh of relief from Parrish, looks of trepidation from the Amaldach-bre women and airs of contentment from the two holy men, the crowd emerged from the forests shade into the warm sunlight and moved out onto the wide open space that was the Gathering Point.

It hadn't changed one bit, decided Parrish as he looked about, standing motionless for as moment. He still faced east, the trees at his back. To his left in a single huge sweeping curve flowed the river Kennet, a gently shelving shallow on the inside of the bend with a steep two meter high bank on the far side. A span of just over twenty five meters of deep, flowing water separated the two.

Opposite to the river ran a long line of upright timbers driven deep into the ground. This formed a fence that linked the two curving ends of the rivers great horseshoe shaped bend, which effectively cordoned off the vast open ground between them and the water. Last time Parrish had been here the space had thronged with perhaps a dozen different tribes of the southern people, all gathered for the annual worship and the chance to trade. Now, as he scanned the deserted openness, it seemed twice as big with just he and his band in it. His eyes were naturally drawn towards the large round hut set exactly in the centre of the line of posts, straddling it to form an obvious gateway. The building had more than one entrance and inside it, he knew, was another huge effigy of the Earth Goddess which everyone paid their respects to before emerging on the far side. Beyond was the start of the long, stone lined avenue that led eventually to Avebury itself.

There appeared to be no waiting reception committee so he settled his people quite near to the riverbank and detailed some of the women to gather firewood and ready a meal for everyone. Only then did he set off with the two village holy men towards the shrine hut. His immediate intention was to make his way towards the causewayed camp of Windmill Hill, beyond the great stone circle, for that was where the holy ones lived.

About three meters short of the hut entrance, impenetrably black against the bright sunshine, he stopped, sensing someone near. Sure enough, right on cue two holy men from the village on the hill emerged into the light. They both wore their ceremonial robes of flowers and feathers. The pair that already accompanied Parrish bowed respectfully to their counterparts, who bowed back before turning to face Parrish and bow deeply to him. He didn't think he deserved such an accolade but bowed briefly back anyway.

Without a single word they offered him the entrance of the hut and he walked on, aware of everyone's eyes on his back.

Once past the central statue and out again into the daylight on the far side the holy men positioned themselves in pairs on either side of him and in a line they walked with respectful silence along the avenue.

It was about two kilometres to the entrance of the great stone circle and the entire distance was travelled without a single word being spoken. Parrish didn't mind in the least. It was nice not to have to make small talk, something he felt the holy men of the times had never mastered, such was their commitment to their religion, and anyway he liked to look at the standing stones, marvelling at their size and form, the preciseness of their positioning and the huge amounts of time and effort that must have gone into their erection.

On the approach to the huge stone circle of Avebury the little troupe turned left along a well worn pathway, passed through a line of trees and on up a gentle incline between the crop fields that's produce helped sustain the people of the village that was now visible above them.

It was the archaeologists of the nineteenth century who had christened it Windmill Hill, finding so many important artefacts there that any other finds in southern England that could be dated to the same period became known by the same name. Thus that certain period of pre-history around 5500-5000BC and the people/culture attached to it became universally known as the period of the Windmill Hill people.

The village had the usual palisade wall around its perimeter and a defence ditch, all be it somewhat shallower than the ones at either Danebury or Hambledon Hill. What made the village so different though was the raised causeway that linked the main village to what amounted to a smaller one alongside. This housed the holy ones and the truly enormous shrine hut of their own. Its thatched conical roof towered up into the sky, much higher than any other dwelling and Parrish suspected it to be the largest hut anywhere in the Neolithic country. He likened its size to the difference between a modern Christian church in comparison to a normal house.

They entered the village through its main gate, passing among the regular sized huts and carried on up onto the causeway. The normal people of the village just glanced up in curiosity as they passed. They had long since abandoned bowing to every single holy man that passed by. At first it seemed somehow irreverent but it didn't take long to come to the conclusion that if this were not so the people who lived here would do nothing but bow all day!

Up on the causeway Parrish was the only man tall enough to see over the wall and looked back down to where they had come from. It was possible to seem very many miles in every direction from this fine vantage point. He noticed with interest that there appeared to be no other villages at all in sight of Windmill Hill, even right out to the far horizon.

On entering the village of the holy ones Parrish also noted, without surprise, that it was devoid of most 'normal' village things. There were no cooking fires, drying kilns, work areas of storage pits.

He knew the people of the main village supported their religious leaders. What did surprise him though, was that instead of being led into the giant shrine hut, as on his only other visit here, he was steered gently away towards one of the more normal sized ones. All five men ducked through its low doorway and Parrish found himself inside a basic dwelling, no different to any of those in his own village, apart from the apparent lack of any cooking facilities.

The whole floor area was covered with those protective woven mats found throughout life in a Neolithic village and sitting on the floor in the centre of them all, well illuminated by tallow lamps, waited a grey haired old man. He too wore bright, colourful flowing robes, as did the holy men who flanked him on both sides.

This man, frail looking and old even by Parrish's twentieth century standards, which made him positively ancient in Neolithic eyes, looked at first glance to be doddery and decrepit, his gently relaxed features giving the impression of advanced senility. Yet nothing could be further from the truth, a fact to which Parrish could well testify, having had first-hand experience of the old man's keen eye and razor sharp mind.

The old one struggled slowly to his feet, shunning the immediate offers of assistance from those beside him, and stepped forward to greet his visitor. His dark eyes, shining beneath the shocks of unruly grey hair that were trying, for the most part successfully, to escape from under his hat, had lost none of their zest for life, glittering with sharp intelligence and some private amusement. He recalled with relish his last meeting with the tall warrior from far flung times.

Parrish too remembered their first meeting. His personal story was known to this, the oldest of the wise ones. Just how he knew was beyond the twentieth century man's comprehension but even so Parrish felt drawn to him. He had instantly liked, respected and trusted this old man. No explanation was necessary. In the end it didn't matter how, it was enough that he just knew!

Parrish stepped forward and met the holy man half way, towering above the grey head. The old man looked up at him and by way of a welcome offered a gentle smile. Parrish grinned back then bowed formally in respect.

"Come. Come and sit with me." came the instantly familiar and unforgettable parchment dry, rustly voice.

Together they sat, this time the old man accepting the offers of help from his assistants. Then they all, as if in response to some unseen signal, drifted away, right to the back of the hut, affording the seated pair in the canter some degree of space and privacy.

"I was glad when you accepted the position of Chieftain at Dane-bre. It was the right thing." He patted Parrish almost affectionately on the knee. "But that is not all. You have been very busy my tall friend."

"Yes." Parrish wondered briefly if he meant with all his killings, or taking care of the widowed women. Perhaps he meant both? Either way, he still intended to do what he could for those who were suffering because of his actions. He jumped in with both feet. "I have all the women of Amaldach-bre with me. They want to know what the future holds for them."

"And what have you offered them?"

Parrish was momentarily struck by the diplomacy of the deceptively simple sounding question. Searching out the options without any prior commitment. After almost two years of Neolithic bluntness of statement it was the last thing he expected.

"Well ..." he stuttered, his confidence shaken. "I ... er ... I told them that if your lot... ah, the holy ones, were agreeable then they could live in your main village. You know, help with the chores, crops, help support Dannu's men ... " He suddenly found himself struggling, trying to justify his reasoning to this so reasonable looking man. He couldn't understand it. Usually he was so sure of himself and yet every time he came face to face with this seemingly harmless old bugger he turned into a gibbering wreck. Of course he knew this man held the greatest power in the land. His word was absolutely final, above and beyond even that of any great, battle hardened Chieftain let alone an outsider from a different time.

The old one let him squirm for just a second longer then once more patted him reassuringly, this time on the shoulder.

"Your choice is a wise one Parrish. It will surely help this place. We would be more than grateful of so many extra willing hands to serve Dannu and, as you say, their lives would then still have worth. Besides, I do not think the Earth Goddess would look too kindly on us if we turned away so many of her daughters in their time of need."

Parrish heaved a great sigh of relief. All his mistakes and then his efforts to rectify them had not been for nothing.

"Thank you. I am grateful for your wise decision."

The old man waved a gnarled and weather beaten hand

dismissively in the air and looked into his companion's eyes.

"Is there anything else you would wish to speak with me about?" he asked almost coyly.

"Er ... no. Not really." Parrish felt the pressure in the old one's eyes.

"Not just now, eh?" He patted the tall man's shoulder again, expecting no reply and getting none. "Then you had better go and tell your people." He added.

"Yes." said Parrish gratefully and jumped to his feet, now glad to have the chance to get out from under the old man's all-seeing eye.

"Before you go ..." The crusty old voice stopped Parrish in his tracks. He turned slowly and looked down at the holy one, something that the man didn't seem to mind in the least.

"Yes?"

"As Chieftain of Dane-bre," for some reason that made him smile, "I would ask if you would attend a ceremony we will shortly hold."

"Ceremony?"

"Yes. It is for your young apprentice holy man. The boy must be formally introduced to the Earth Goddess and I would like it if you were there also."

"Me? Why?"

"Because he will be your next holy man when your friend here is gone."

He indicated briefly to the Dane-bre holy man who still stood silently in the shadows behind. There was no emotion on the man's face at the prediction of his eventual death. "And because I also feel that you might benefit from it."

"Of course I will attend. It would be a great honour." The words were out of Parrish's' mouth before he could stop them. "When?"

"Soon. Now go and tend to your people." The seated holy man nodded to the door. "I look forward to seeing you again."

His final act was to dismiss the tall man with another wave of his hand and Parrish bowed once more then quickly ducked out of the hut to stand once again in the sunshine. A few moments later his own holy man emerged, clearly intending to accompany his Chieftain back to the Gathering Point.

Parrish exhaled forcibly. Despite his unexplainable affection for the old man he always felt as if he'd just been grilled after talking with him.

Hah, he thought dryly, the old sod was so sharp that one day he would cut himself if he wasn't careful.

The two Danebury men set off in silence to return to where the women of Amaldach-bre and his own warriors, no doubt still being pampered, waited for news.

As he walked away from the village it suddenly occurred to Parrish that this was the second time he had met and talked with the wisest of the wise ones. And yet he still didn't even know his name!

18

When Parrish broke the news to the women of Amaldach-bre, that they were of that village no more, there were sighs of relief and much excited chatter from among them. The women of Dane-bre were very pleased for their new friends and grateful to their Chieftain for his wise decisions and their fruitful conclusions. Once again it seemed that no matter how strange the situation, he always seemed to do the right thing. The warriors remained aloof from these womanly dealings but were also proud of their Chieftain. The confirmation of his earlier predictions, made back in Dane-bre, showed without question his great wisdom.

Now it was plain that the two groups were to part, and only one warrior approached his Chieftain and requested a wife from among the women they had escorted. The man in question had lost one of his two wives to pneumonia the previous winter. As was proper, Parrish took the man to one side, making a big show of the fact that they would now need to discuss her price.

When they were alone Parrish declared to the humbled warrior that he had no real need of material goods, those things he could acquire simply by request, but he was always ready to learn more of a warrior's ways and skills. Thus, if the man felt he could be of help with any knowledge if they were ever out hunting together, he would be happy if the warrior could use this to repay his debt. Perhaps pointing out animal sign his Chieftain might have missed or explain any pieces of woodland lore that he felt to be useful. The tall man would be satisfied to take his payment from the man in the form of information.

Of course the warrior was only too happy to agree to the terms. It would be an honour. In fact he would have readily volunteered the information if he had but known his Chieftain so desired it. But then he realized it was his clever Chieftains way of learning more without directly having to ask and then appear not to be all knowing. In truth all the warriors knew that Parrish still did not understand many of the ways of mortal men. Was that not the very reason he had befriended Klud? Yet the Chieftain had now put it to this simple, honest warrior of his village in such a way that if he offered up information it would appear that the man could just take it on board only if he so wished. That way no one on either side would be seen to lose face.

The deal was gladly struck with respectful bows and both parties happy with their lot, and so another person entered the tribe of the village of Dane-bre.

As far as all the other ladies went, each knew they were now destined to live up on Windmill Hill. Young Tomps never approached Parrish about a second wife, much to the disappointment of several women.

Parrish respected the youngster's decision and never raised the subject, wondering if the lad had that much respect for his own wife. Karin in turn wondered if her great Chieftain had perhaps had quiet words with her husband. Tomps himself never considered a second woman because his friend, his hero, his Chieftain, had never needed more than one wife. If that were good enough for the tall man, then it was certainly more than good enough for him!

Parrish knew that it was not the done thing for a Chieftain to explain his actions and so simply informed his warrior band that they would be staying at the Gathering Point for a few days more before setting off home. His people never pondered much on the announcement, just immediately began organizing themselves to the task of making shelters as protection from the elements. There was no need for a hunting party, he pointed out to his men. For the few days they remained, their food would be provided by the people of the village of the holy ones. This received nods of satisfaction from both the warriors and their wives, all who saw it as a release from at least one of the daily chores.

The little Danebury camp thus moved a bit further away from the edge of the river Kennet now it was to become slightly more permanent, simply to avoid harassment from the early summer midges that swarmed along its bank in the evenings. As another aid to comfort Parrish also informed his people that if the weather turned really bad and it rained hard, they had his permission to take shelter from any downpour inside the gateway hut behind them. He was sure Dannu would not mind.

Everyone bent willingly to their new tasks and Parrish felt suddenly redundant, forced to watch the work going on while doing none himself. Menial tasks were done for him by his men. It did at least give him some satisfaction to see both Klud and Tomps take a personal interest in the building of the simple structure that would be his own. Juli could do nothing but stand helplessly by as the men set to work and, despite his self disgust at how he had let his wife down, he found himself smiling at the way she was being served by the two warriors. How he admired both man and boy. It filled him with warmth. He knew a man with friends like his was rich beyond avarice.

One man who took full advantage of the opportunity afforded him by a few enforced days of idleness was the Danebury holy man. He had some urgent catching up to do. From someone in the Windmill Hill village he had obtained one of those special, patterned clay cups filled with the blue/black dye and began to visit the warriors in turn. He stopped them in their labours for the more important task of tattooing. It was not considered a hindrance to the men. They were proud to suffer the agonies of the cutting flint. The extra circles cut on the necks of those who had earned them were proud statements of their battle honours.

The only man to refuse this 'service', and secretly the holy man was not too surprised, was the Chieftain himself. Firstly he would not accept the offer of marks for the nine men he had murdered as they slept. They were not killed in an honourable fight and Parrish would not make glory of that. And as for Tanis, his skull was already on display in the Chieftains stall but Parrish told the holy man bluntly that he would not give the red bearded wife beater the satisfaction of being an honourable trophy mark on his neck.

As the body count was done and the battle marks meted out it came as a bit of a surprise to everyone that neither Parrish nor Klud had a single head to their own credit. Neither seemed the least bit perturbed by this revelation. In those first exchanges of fire across that New Forest clearing it seemed that not one man had been hit. Parrish deliberately omitted to mention to anyone the men he knew had fallen to his traps, and no one knew just how many had died in the river Avon. Klud alone knew of these events and although he did not understand the reasons, respected his Chieftains silence on the matter and said nothing.

And so, once more many warriors of Danebury sported proud and for a while sore necks, displaying the honours of battle once again bestowed upon them by the actions of their Chieftain. When the tattooing was at last finished the little shaman too sighed in satisfaction. He knew that there were still more men to be seen to once he got back to Dane-bre, for only half of the men who fought were here now, but it felt good to be doing his proper work once more. It didn't matter that he did not fight himself, he was just as proud of his village and its achievements as the next man.

Two days later Parrish found himself being shaken awake by his holy man. After a brief moment to gain his bearings he sat up, rubbing the sleep from his eyes. It was very early and still dark, a crisp clear night with a myriad of bright stars winking almost knowingly down from the blackness above.

"Now?" asked Parrish quietly.

The holy man nodded. Parrish understood. He had experienced this once before. The last time it had happened there had followed a torchlight procession, with the villagers of the south land's gathering together en mass and walking out through the last of the night to meet the dawn at the temple of Dannu.

He turned briefly away from the little shaman and glanced down at Juli, laying quiet beside him. She was awake he saw, her bright eyes glittered in the darkness, but she had not moved. His first instinct was to pat her reassuringly on the shoulder before leaving but he checked his arm, leaving the gesture of affection undone.

After pulling on his boots, lacing them swiftly up and gathering up his jacket for protection against the early morning nip, he jumped to his feet, all the time the holy man waiting in patient silence. He shrugged the garment on, fell in alongside the small man and together they set off towards the gate hut.

The shaman ushered him in, past the shadow shrouded statue and on out the other side to the start of the stone avenue. The sight there took him momentarily aback and he stopped to take in the spectacle.

Gathered together, illuminated by the dancing lights of many blazing torches, stood all the younger holy ones of Windmill Hill, each man dressed in his religious finery. Parrish turned in time to see his own shaman adjusting the hat of his own clothes. He had already donned his cape and only then did Parrish realize that he too wore his official regalia, tasselled leg bands and all.

This was not as before and the Chieftain opened his mouth to ask but all the little shaman did was point, redirecting the tall man's gaze into the middle of the crowd. At its centre, clearly overawed by the whole occasion, was the young lad who had been chosen to succeed the Danebury priest.

Parrish grasped it all then. This was to be some sort of a dry run. A practice procession for the benefit of the boy. He needed to learn the responsibilities required at these religious ceremonies. Yes, that was it, and now they would all proceed to the great stone circle and do whatever it was that holy men did among the stones. No doubt the youngster would be lectured and instructed on the niceties and nuances that a holy one of a village must be aware of during the times of worship for those of his people. Those villagers that would eventually be under his care and guidance when he became their spiritual leader.

Parrish could see that to one so young it must all seem a huge and daunting responsibility. As for himself, no doubt he was just along for the ride, probably required to be there as Chieftain of the village the apprentice was one day to inherit. He relaxed. Clearly he was just a casual observer of this event. Now that he knew he was not expected to participate personally his own tension eased and he smiled broadly at the waiting crowd. With an almost magnanimous 'carry on' gesture of his arms he signalled for the young men to continue their prehistoric induction. Reacting to his action as if it were a starting signal, as one the crowd turned and set off along the avenue away from the Gathering Point. Parrish fell in once more, this time at the rear, and watched with intent as they paraded through the dark, many individual holy men approaching the lad in turn and speaking with him. It seemed his time to learn had truly begun.

"What are they saying?" Parrish whispered to the Danebury shaman after watching the ritual for a while.

"There is no need for you to know." replied the little man rather arrogantly. "But there are many things *he* will need to understand and it will take many years for him to know them. But this is part of his work for Dannu that will be clearly seen by his villagers and so it is right that he learn this first."

Fair point, thought Parrish, for once not to annoyed at not getting a satisfactory answer to his question. He had no real wish to understand the intricacies of the holy rites of worship to the Earth Goddess anyway. It was enough to understand that if the apprentice was as good, as true and as conscientious as his predecessor then Parrish, as Chieftain, would have no cause for complaint.

The false dawn was beginning to show as the straggly entourage finally approached the greatest stone circle of them all. As before when Parrish had been there, they filed respectfully into the huge monument. All then circled the central stone arrangement and stood in silence watching the more senior of the holy one's present gather about the central altar stone. Daylight was all but upon them now and as the sun began to rise all the holy men began to chant, the lad joining in hesitantly at first but with rapidly growing confidence. Parrish was the only man there silent although he was now filled with a heightening sense of anticipation. The last time he'd seen this particular ritual, when the sunlight finally hit the stone an amazing thing happened.

This time though the tall man was to be disappointed. As before, the chanting grew louder and more insistent, reaching its rousing climax before cutting sharply off with perfect timing just as the first rays touched the altar stone. But nothing happened. The holy men simply waited in silence for a few minutes as the strain of their exertions eased away and the sun rose fully above the high, white chalked bank that surrounded Avebury. Then they slowly reformed into their rough processional line and began to file back out of the temple.

"Was that it?!" said Parrish incredulously, knowing all along that it had been a dry run, yet still deeply disappointed. He had hoped to see that special something again this fine morning.

"Patience, Parrish." said the Holy man with a sly, knowing look in his eye. "There is yet more to come."

"Oh." was the rather sheepish reply and, once again but now in total silence, the entourage set off. Not back to the Gathering Point though. This time they headed along the pathway that skirted the religious site, the one leading inescapably up towards the causewayed camp that squatted low on the brow of the hill above them.

19

They all entered the gate to the main village and Parrish was surprised to see the entire 'civilian' population of Windmill Hill in attendance, lining the central pathway that led through the encampment and up onto the causeway. As the procession passed them by the people bowed deeply and it suddenly became clear that they were all showing their respect to the young boy at the centre of the event. It impressed Parrish that he took all the silent adulation with great aplomb, just bowing his head occasionally, sometimes directing the nod if he caught an individual's eye. Not once though did he smile.

Up onto the causeway the procession went, Parrish taking another opportunity to examine briefly the Neolithic countryside around them, then on into the camp of the holy men. This time everyone knew where they were going and without need of direction they all filed into the entrance of the truly huge shrine hut. It led into a dim tunnel, lit only with a few, evenly spaced tallow lamps. As the men entered the portal they began to chant softly, the unintelligible words echoing back and forth in the confined space. The tunnel sloped gently downward, its exit showing more brightly lit ahead of them, where Parrish knew it emerged into the central base of the building.

The procession emerged into the brighter light and now stood in the shrine hut proper, their quiet chant taking on new dimensions as it immediately benefited both from the rather astounding acoustics of the great conical shaped construction work and the additional voices of what Parrish took to be the more senior holy men already seated and waiting inside. The men of the procession peeled away as they emerged and, with the deftness that comes with familiarity, they mounted the graded, evenly stepped levels until they found their own places.

The whole place was like a crude Roman amphitheatre, three quarters of the circular hut filled to the back with this shelving system, each level one higher and one more back, all the way out to the wall. If the seating arrangements represented some form hierarchy among the religious order Parrish didn't know, but he never dwelt on the subject. There were other things now to consider.

Directly in front of him across the space of the floor Parrish recognized the oldest of the old ones. The grey haired man beckoned him across the stark openness with a wave of his hand and Parrish complied, moving up to stand on his left in the space seemingly provided especially for him. In the time it took to do this all the others had also found their places and so the twentieth century man was the last person to turn and face the object that totally dominated the interior. Towering up above them, the tunnels exit directly at its feet, was an immense statue of the Earth Goddess.

She was at least eight meters high and her total weight was anybody's guess. But this was no time for technical details, she was now there simply to be stared at! The skilfully sculpted stonework was illuminated by dozens of strategically placed tallow lamps that used their constantly flickering light to give the smooth, rounded surfaces an odd kind of sheen. Vaguely hypnotic as an almost pulsating, living effect came back through the light, somehow reminiscent of the pulsing veins beneath the skin of a bare body, the life blood coursing through them.

Standing below the statue, directly between it and Parrish and the old one, was the young apprentice. He faced the huge effigy with unconcealed nervousness, head tilted right back as he looked up at her. The Chieftain of Danebury dragged his eyes from the spectacle and turned to say something to the man beside him but was held to silence by a single raised finger. Casually looking up past the man to the rest of the hut's occupiers, Parrish was suddenly aware of everyone else in the building, on all levels, staring fixedly at the statue. Some almost looked trancelike in their expressions. At that moment the ever present chanting began to increase in volume and intensity, the echoing acoustics reverberating and enhancing this suddenly all invading sound. Like those throbbing drums played in his own village shrine hut at times of celebration, the noise went right into Parrish's head and vibrated through his body, the overriding feeling one of a tingling buzz from some deep seated vibration.

As if he were being turned by the shoulders by guiding hands, the action not consciously one of his own doing, he swivelled to once again face the statue. All the while the noise continued to increase. To compound things even further, now coming from all the holy men behind him like an almost tangible pressure on the back of his neck, he sensed a wave if intense concentration. As the chant increased still more the feeling increased too until it was as if he were being physically pushed from behind. Urged by willing thoughts towards the Earth Goddess.

But he could not move. His eyes were locked onto the statue of Dannu. The illumination around it seemed to be getting brighter. And still brighter. His skin tingled unnaturally and, although unable to pull his eyes from the statue, he managed with some effort to raise his hands into the edge of his vision. To his astonishment they were swathed in a faint bluish glow. His first thought on seeing it was of Saint Elmo's fire and yet he knew that it was not. Judging by how the rest of his skin felt just the same as his hands, he knew his whole body must be shrouded in the faint aura.

Then he jolted, hit by what felt like an electrical charge of some magnitude, and went completely rigid, pulled up onto his toes by the pain. In fact all the holy men in the hut were being similarly affected to a greater or lesser degree.

Parrish was unaware of all this. He felt pinned like a butterfly collector's specimen, unable to move away from the pain or avert his eyes from the statue. It now glowed very brightly, its harsh glare increasing constantly until in just a few seconds more it was so bright it began to hurt his eyes. But still he could not look away or even close his eyes, drawn up into the light until it filled his head and he could not see at all. Just an endless sea of blinding whiteness.

The pain was such that he wanted to cry out but the shout died on his lips, turned in an instant to a gasp of amazement. From out of the dazzle a figure slowly emerged, coming closer until it was floating just beyond his focus. The light blurred its edges and made it difficult to identify, but he was sure it was there all right.

A woman. He felt sure it was a woman and that she meant him no harm. He couldn't explain how he knew, he just did. As if to confirm this she offered out a hand to him in friendship. The pain was momentarily forgotten as Parrish all at once felt an overwhelming urge to go to her but could not, pinned as he was by his own aura, rigid in every joint and muscle. Somehow the woman knew he would have gone to her if he could and it was very plain that she would have welcomed him. The warmth there was unmistakable. Even with the indistinctness of her features, blurred as they were by the intensity of the whiteness, Parrish saw the smile. A smile to warm the heart of any man.

Strangely, it instantly reminded him of how Juli used to smile at him.

Seemingly satisfied with the reaction to her gesture, the figure nodded then slowly drew back from the tall man, back into the all enveloping light until she was gone from sight. Parrish didn't want her to leave but was powerless to stop her and unexplainably felt a sharp pang of sadness when she was gone.

Like the extinguishing of a powerful arc lamp, the light was abruptly gone. It's absence momentarily blinded Parrish almost as much as its former brightness and he jerked back, slumping momentarily into the arms of the old one who stood ready beside him. He was helped gently down onto the seating platform behind them. The same thing was happening to certain others of the holy men all around the hut and almost at the twentieth century man's feet, totally stunned by his own experience, the young apprentice lay prostrate on the floor but was now being attended to.

Parrish quickly regained his equilibrium, fought off the helping hands and sat up, rubbing his eyes to try and rid them of the dancing greenness that obscured his vision.

"What the fuck was all that!?" he gasped in English, then shrugged his shoulders and rubbed the small of his back as the after effects of being stretched taught in every muscle washed over him. Every sinew in his body felt used.

"That hurt." This time he spoke the language of his people.

"Yes." said he old man, now sitting somewhat more attentively beside him, a knowing smile on his face. "The experience does not come without its own price."

Parrish took a long moment to look around at the other holy men. They now all sat quiet and composed in their respective places, drawn faces the only sign that others had experienced what he just had. He was both shocked by the whole astounding event and impressed by the priest's apparent powers of recovery. Didn't they too feel as if they had just been plugged into the mains?

The young lad who was at the centre of this amazing event was now on his feet. He too looked tired but resting easily on his young features was a soft, satisfied grin. No need for him to say that he was happy now and no longer unsure of his future. He was more than satisfied to know that his chosen path through life could hold such rich rewards.

At a signal from the old one the boy led off up the tunnel and out of the shrine hut. The others began to follow. A soft song sprung up from the departing priests, almost spontaneously it seemed although Parrish never doubted that it was also part of the ceremony, a song of gratitude and loyalty.

The grey haired old man patted Parrish on the knee and spoke quietly.

"Wait a while my friend, sit with me."

And so the tall man sat in silence, sharply aware of the occasional curious glances being shot in his direction as the rest of the holy men filed past on their way out.

"Why are they staring at me?" he whispered from the side of his mouth.

"You were very open to it." came the rather non explanatory reply. "More so than some who have worshipped for many years."

Parrish fell silent again, pondering on the answer until the hut was finally empty. Now it was just him, the old man and the giant statue. He turned to quiz the wise one but was beaten to the punch by that rustly old voice.

"What did you see?" he was asked quietly.

"I ... I saw ..." There was a long pause.

"Her." The holy man finished the sentence for him. Parrish shrugged. He could find no words of explanation.

"It is all right my young friend." said the holy man in a soft, reassuring voice. He could well understand how overawed by it all he must be. "You were honoured."

At that Parrish scoffed. He knew he was a man with no honour and said so bitterly.

"You do not know the things I have done, old man. I do not deserve those words."

"I know what has happened. And I know what you think." He looked into the tall man's eyes and held them with his own, piercing gaze. "Only you, I and Dannu know of your other life and that my friend is where your trouble lies. I tell you now Parrish that you are wrong.

Here it is not important how you see yourself. It is enough that here the people, your people, believe in you. They believe in your righteousness, your honesty and your good intentions." He paused momentarily, stopping short of also saying that the same people also believed him to be Dannu's man.

"If you see yourself as dishonoured, then it is you who see falsely. Do not shut yourself away from those who need and respect you. Reach out to the people in your care and embrace them and their goodwill toward you.

If you also think you must 'put right' the wrong you believe you have done, then look back my son at your past deeds and see how good they have been. How right for those you did them for. How *honourable.*

As for your child's death, do not blame Dannu. It was not her wish for that to happen but you more than anyone must know that men do bad here, as well as good. The Earth Goddess guides each person towards their destiny. She does not control what they do along their road, just shows them the way, as she has done to you.

I tell you now that for the untimely death of your son *you* did not take revenge on the men of Amaldach-bre. You were just the instrument of Dannu's revenge!"

Parrish had up to that moment been listening in passive silence but the words about his dead son went deep. And yet as soon as the old one spoke that last sentence an odd recollection sprang suddenly into his head. How many times had he been warned by his own holy man that to offend the Earth Goddess was to invite swift and terrible retribution? How, had never been explained. Perhaps he now knew!

"You must not punish yourself too much, Parrish." The old one patted him once more on the knee. "For it is by now well known that you have done well for the lost ones of Amaldach-bre. Your task is very nearly complete. But there is one last thing to be done before it is over and you can return to the path of your destiny."

"Yes!" exclaimed Parrish. The cry was not so much one of acknowledgment as one of understanding. The great words just spoken, true words, suddenly made him realize that he had done the best he could. Although he could not deny that there was occasionally some terrible evil done in this land, it was vastly outweighed by the goodness, righteousness and honour that flowed like sweet wine out of the people who worshipped the Earth Goddess and respected her land and her word. He knew these people and knew it was so.

The great weight of the burden of guilt suddenly lifted from his shoulders. His relief was immense, the feeling washing refreshingly over him and bringing with it the return of his essential drive and energy, that irrepressible love of life, the power of it revitalizing him in both heart and mind.

In an instant he knew what this last task was. He had made peace with himself, now he must make his peace with the one other person he had inflicted pain upon.

"You are right old man." he said, jumping eagerly to his feet. "I must see Juli at once and put right the terrible wrong I have done to her."

He spun on his heel, a true smile on his face for the first time in a long while, and sped off up the tunnel without so much as an acknowledging glance towards the statue of the Earth Goddess or a farewell gesture to the old man.

The wise one sighed sadly, shaking his head, then looked up into the face of Dannu, shrugged and said quietly.

"I tried. But it was foretold by you that he would not stay to listen."

20

The Gathering Point was buzzing with the throng of Danebury people, all there among the two peer groups still discussing the possible purpose of their Chieftains call to the village of the holy ones.

Everyone of course knew that there was some kind of mysterious event due to happen concerning the young successor to their village holy man, and the current rumour was that Parrish must have had something to do with it. Some kind of involvement yes, although just on what level they could only guess. It made sense. After all, was he not Dannu's man? It must surely follow then that he would be required in the joining between the Earth Goddess and the young shaman to be of his own village. Some read it to as another good omen from Dannu for the continuing prosperity of the village of Dane-bre.

When Parrish came striding purposefully back through the gate hut towards the cluster of his waiting people they all turned to him in barely disguised curiosity but if they were expecting some kind of explanation or other kind words they were mistaken. He walked silently through the gathered warriors, who parted before him, and on towards the huddled group of women. They all bowed their heads respectfully as he approached. Parrish stepped straight up to his wife.

"Juli." He said. Quiet, but purposeful.

Her head lifted and their eyes met briefly before she remembered and cast them down again. It had been impossible for her to read what lay within their depths. That famous piercing gaze of his was as strong but still as passive as ever.

"I would speak with you alone. Come."

Without waiting for or expecting an answer he spun on his heel and headed off towards the gap between the trees that led out of the Gathering Point. Juli could do nothing more than follow quietly, a few paces behind.

Once they were out of earshot speculation began again in earnest among those who were left behind for a second time.

It was very nearly summer and the sun was now rising steadily into the morning sky and spreading its warming rays upon the land. Lancing through any gaps in the broadleaf canopy, the bright beams highlighted gently swooping insects that flitted and hovered among the towering trunks, and fell upon the forest floor, richly carpeted with mosses, ferns and the occasional cluster of woodland flowers, bright dollops of colour on a broad green canvas.

Parrish led Juli through all this natural loveliness until they came to a quiet, secluded, grass carpeted clearing. The light here at its centre, unobstructed by foliage, was brighter and warmer and they both stood for a few moments, adjusting to it.

Finally Parrish faced his diminutive wife, looked down on her with a fondness he knew would stay with him always, and with a voice that was full of regret, said softly.

"I know you are my wife. I know you do not care for me anymore, but I just want you to know too that for all the pain I have caused you, and for the loss of the baby, I am truly, truly sorry."

He hung his head in shame, looking down at his scuffed and dirty boots. They looked just how he felt.

In reaction to his words Juli simply looked up at him in wonderment. Chieftains never apologized. Warriors never apologized. Husbands never apologized. But he just had, and to a mere woman too!!

"I ... I do not understand." she stammered, the amazement clear on her face.

"I know you do not care for me now," he said slowly, almost choking on the words it hurt so much for him to say. "For I was not there to protect you. When you needed my protection most. And because of that our son was lost. I do not blame you for hating me. I just wanted you to know that I am so very sorry for my failures, and for hurting you so much."

"Oh, Parrish." she gasped. "How could you think such a thing?"

The unexpected question brought the tall man's head up and he gazed intently into her eyes. How they shone in the sunlight.

"Because it is true." he said quietly.

Juli shook her head and then did what would normally be considered an unforgivable thing. She corrected a warrior. Worse, she corrected a Chieftain.

"No. That is not true." Never had she been so sure of a statement.

"Huh?" He blurted out that ignorant sounding grunt she like so much.

"My husband, it is I who am sorry." she whispered. "I denied Tanis and so it was me who lost your son. I know how much the baby meant to you. I saw how much the loss hurt you. I knew then that you would never care for me again. But I am still your wife," she hurried on before he could interrupt, determined now to say what needed to be said, before her nerve failed her. "and I will take care of you until the day I die. And I will do it gladly, it is my honour."

Parrish stood in stunned silence for several long moments after she had finished. Juli began to tremble. She was well aware that she had gone too far and been much too outspoken. There were surely to be severe retributions for her unforgivable outburst, but she would not shirk from any punishment he might administer. She had at last said what she felt needed to be said.

Her tall husband stepped up close and she couldn't help it, she flinched as he reached out for her, but to her surprise all he did was gather her into his arms and hold her to him. Slowly, cautiously at first, she reached out too. Her arms snaked around his waist and there, in the middle of Dannu's forest, they hugged each other.

"Juli, Juli, Juli." he whispered. "What fools we have been. I thought that you did not care for me and you thought I did not care for you. All that pain and sorrow. If only we had talked sooner. Oh, I am still so sorry for the loss of our son, but at least now I have my wife back." He raised his eyes to the sky. Thank Dannu, he added in a silent whisper.

Juli pulled back from his arms to say that it was still her fault the baby had died before he had even lived, but stopped dead when she looked into her husband's face. The smile was unmistakable, that rare smile that she normally only saw when they used to lay together. But what took her breath away was the look in his eyes and the single tear that escaped that very moment from the corner of his eye, to run unchecked down his cheek.

Her heart went out to him then and a lump came to her throat. Never had she seen such a thing from a warrior. It seemed to the Neolithic girl that Parrish would forever be the master of the unexpected and astounding. He would always amaze, surprise and impress her. She just worshiped him. With a gentle hand she wiped away the glistening tear and smiled up at the tall man in her arms. A great man. Dannu's man. Her Chieftain. Her husband.

"Do not cry." she said in a warm, hushed tone. "We are together again and I am sure, if it is the will of Dannu, there will be other chances for babies."

Parrish could not speak, so choked was he with emotion. He just nodded and held her close once more. This time Juli hugged him so tight, as if she never, ever wanted to let him out of her arms again, feeling almost desperate now to show to her husband just how much she cared for him.

"Parrish?" Her voice was still quiet.

"Mmm ...?"

"Would now be one of those chances?" She held her breath in anticipation of his answer.

He held her away once more and gazed down at her, a softer smile on his face.

"Are you sure?"

He felt he didn't want to push his good fortune. After all, as far as he was concerned they had only just become man and wife again. Mind you, he considered as the realization gripped him, what better time? Juli nodded as if reading his thoughts.

"Yes." she said breathlessly. "I want your seed."

"It would be my honour." he said slowly, then grinned and bowed to her, a gesture he thought complementarily but she took with some confusion. She did not deserve such respect. A man never bowed like that to a woman. And yet she knew that he really meant it.

He started to undo his jacket but she put her tiny hands on his.

"Let me." she said softly.

Parrish held his hands away from his sides in a gesture of submission and she undressed him, only accepting help to remove his boots and tug off his trousers.

Then he was naked, standing hard and proud in the middle of the small forest glade, the rays of the sun warming his skin and the love for his wife warming his heart. He felt no embarrassment. In fact nothing felt more right as he bared himself body and soul to his wife beneath the all seeing eye of the Earth Goddess.

Juli drank in the contours of his muscular frame with her eyes as she shucked out of her own clothing. It always amazed Parrish just how quickly she could do it.

She stepped clear of the jumbled pile of cloth around her feet and went to her husband, hugging him in pure pleasure. She loved to feel her bare skin against his and was well aware of his manhood, pushing with hard urgency against her.

Parrish lowered himself to the soft grass and cradled Juli all the way, revelling in the simple closeness of her body in all her glorious nakedness. A great sigh of contentment heaved out of her and she rolled onto her back, welcoming him with open arms.

He lifted himself until he was poised above her, before gently lowering until they were together and holding each other again, and kissed her hard on the mouth, long and lingering. She returned the kiss with passion and, as if this were a sign, Parrish eased himself into her with one long thrust of his hips, until he was fully enveloped. It felt so good!

There was no need for movement then, both satisfied at that moment with the intimate contact between them. For Juli it was heaven enough that she was joined again with her tall husband. Wherever their bodies touched her skin tingled. It was somehow indescribable but gave her such joy. The feelings were unearthly and she knew they were a gift from Dannu, given to her through her man. Parrish was in turn filled with overwhelming joy at the restoration of the closeness with his diminutive wife, something he thought he had lost forever. Being joined with her sent shivers of pleasure washing down his spine like soft waves of electricity.

The happy pair could have stayed just like that for ever, locked together by their passion, but a new urgency took hold of Parrish. He needed to give his seed to Juli as much as he knew she wanted it.

With slow, tingling, muscle aching movements he began to push himself in and out of her. She in turn pushed back against him, matching his rhythm and pulling him even tighter to her body.

In their heightened state of excitement both knew that they would not, could not last very long. Each one wanted the feeling to last forever but each also wanted to reach that magic, marvellous and mystical moment of climax and fulfilment.

Parrish was first to start succumbing to his more primal side and began to increase the speed and power of his thrusts, arching his back with the effort and desire to go as far as he could into his wife's enveloping love, all the time building up towards his peak.

He was shocked as his desire was cut cruelly short when suddenly Juli stopped and pushed her husband away. He couldn't believe how she could do such a thing. Couldn't believe how she could stop him when he was so close, and couldn't believe her control if she too was as close as he. For one terrible moment Parrish thought her action a vicious act of spitefulness. To shut him out at the last minute, a cold and heartless way of getting back at him for the things he had done.

But the look of adoration in her eyes dispelled the bad thought. Juli simply wished to give her husband as much joy as she could muster and make these unrepeatable moments last. And she knew how.

Now she dared to take control and bring him to his peak at *her* speed, knowing how much he had enjoyed it when she had done the same thing before. Pushing him over onto his back, she climbed astride him and, taking his wet hardness in her hands, guided him into her.

Sitting across his hips with her hands pushing gently on his broad chest, she once more began moving against him, this time her hips pressing down onto his and controlling the speed and movement of his rising.

Parrish laughed for joy, cupped his wife's pert breasts in his hands and let her lead him. The sun bathed their pale bodies in its warmth, bright beams of light rippling across them as it winked almost approvingly down through the high, leafy boughs. At last neither could stand the exquisite denial anymore and as one they swept up to the great crescendo that only true lovers felt.

It was all Juli could do to gasp as she dropped onto her husband's chest, holding him as tight as she possibly could while the feelings without description roared inside her, sweeping her entire being with unbelievable pleasure and power, snatching away her breath.

Parrish in turn clutched his wife to him, arching his back so much at the vital moment that he lifted her clear of the ground, and as his seed thundered into Juli he let out a great cry. A cry of pleasure and satisfaction and fulfilment. A sound that echoed through the forest like the soulful bay of the wild wolf.

The moment was everlasting and yet all too short. The strength of their passion ebbed out of them and they lay back upon the forest floor, happy beyond words. Parrish laughed.

"I was a bit noisy then. Do you think anyone heard?"

"I do not care." said Juli, her soft voice full of contentment. "I would not care if all the people on Dannu's land heard."

He turned his head and gazed at his little Neolithic wife. She looked simply radiant and he thought he had never seen anyone more beautiful.

"Juli." he said softly. "I love you."

The word seemed so short somehow, he thought. A word describing something so wonderful really ought to be much longer at least.

Juli too thought the word strange but for a totally different reason. A puzzled look came over her face and she tried the strange sounding English word on her lips.

"What is 'love'?"

"Er ... " Parrish was totally stumped for a few moments. That was a tough one. He gently stroked his wife's cheek with his fingertips and struggled for a satisfactory answer. At length he said,

"Love is ... caring for someone else more than you care for yourself." He nodded to himself, satisfied with the description.

Juli didn't even need to think over her husband's wise words, as she normally had to. These words she immediately understood. She grinned and kissed him.

"Then I love you too."

Parrish laughed again and hugged her tightly, before suddenly making her squeal as he jerked up into a sitting position and started tickling her.

The way she squirmed with delight, naked and young beneath his hands, was something else he'd almost forgotten how much he enjoyed.

21

When the happy couple returned to the Gathering Point they found the huddle of wickiups that marked the makeshift Danebury camp deserted. All its inhabitants had left the middle of the clearing and were now gathered some fifty meters away at the river's edge.

As they approached the group, all who had their backs turned, Parrish could hear Klud's voice and, sure enough, as he drew closer it became clear that his good friend, who stood right at the river's edge, held centre stage.

"What is this?" he asked casually from just behind the throng, making them all, up till that moment unaware of his approach, start and back away, bowing apologetically. He ignored their embarrassment and joined Klud before his people, the warrior beckoning him forward as soon as he had made his presence known.

"You can tell them now yourself, Parrish." he said loudly. "For I feel that my word alone is not enough!" He pretended to sound insulted but everyone knew it was in jest because clearly the bushy eye browed warrior was enjoying being the centre of attention. He was revelling in the chance to tell one and all about his adventures with their tall Chieftain, in particular the astounding event that he had witnessed and even been a part of, where Dannu and her man had been in close contact.

"Tell them what?"

"How you crossed the deep river without sinking to the bottom and dying. Tell them too how you can move through water although it is impossible to hold onto or push against. And how you carried me across it too, in the palm of one hand!"

"Huh?" grunted Parrish once again, at first unable to make any sense of his friend's words. He looked around at the faces of his people and saw the wonder there. And perhaps too a small hint of disbelief. Then realization dawned and he allowed a small smile to cross his face.

"But it is only 'swimming'." he said finally, shrugging.

"Call it what you will." It was the holy man who spoke then. He did not understand the strange sounding word at the end of the sentence but he did not doubt Klud's word for a moment and, like every other single person now gathered with him, was curious too and very much wanted to see what this 'swimming' was. He put forth the question everyone else was thinking.

"Will you show us how it is done?"

"Yes, show them, my friend." Klud was quick to back up the little shaman.

But Parrish shook his head. This was getting too silly.

"I do not think so."

To his surprise there was a chorus of low groans of disappointment from his people.

They had all hoped to have the chance of witnessing such a thing as had never before been seen. Everyone fell into a disappointed silence. Parrish's gaze travelled from face to face and they all registered the same. Their fervent hope had been dashed by their own leader. He knew he had done nothing wrong yet felt unexplainably guilty and shuffled uncomfortably from one foot to the other. These were the people that he loved and he hated the idea that even on such a small matter as a simple show of skill, he appeared to have let them down. And so, with an air of resignation, he succumbed to their silent demand.

Ah, what the hell, he thought. Clearly they badly wanted to see me swim. I feel good in myself now and besides, the water does look quite inviting.

He shrugged his broad shoulders.

"OK." he said, making the tone of his voice sound as if he had resignedly given in to the wishes of his people against his own. It was partly true although he realized the more he thought about it the more a quick dip appealed. Plus it warmed his heart to see the grins unanimously appear back on the faces of those in his charge. Now their anticipation was plain.

He started to remove his jacket and was helped out of it by willing hands from several of his men. The other warriors nodded in satisfaction at their Chieftains willingness to bow to the wishes of his people. The women all watched as discretely as they could without actually staring.

Everyone was charged with expectancy. Without doubt this was to be a rare treat.

Parrish quickly stripped to the waist, pulled off his boots then stood before the crowd dressed only in his buckskin trousers. Only now self conscious of all eyes on him, he tried to make light of the situation and jokingly struck a bodybuilders pose, flexing his muscles in a parody of Arnold Schwarzenegger and flashing a cheesy grin.

No one laughed.

He still didn't understand that in Neolithic Britain his physique was so much more than everyone else's that to them he *was* a huge, muscled and powerful man. Both warriors and women took the chance of this rare opportunity to examine their strange Chieftain closely for those few seconds before Parrish realized they didn't get the joke.

To the men his skin was too pale for that of a normal full grown man, but for their Chieftain it clearly did not mean ill health. The raggedly scarred neck and arm told of his battle with the wolf pack. The wolf kill tattoo high up on his cheek, the circular rings on his neck and the lines of the bear on his arm now seemed to stand out in stark relief. All these were marks that spoke of greatness.

The women in contrast saw not the signs of victorious battle but the tight, knotted muscles and the towering physique. Those who had been fortunate enough to have washed the mud from his body after he had killed the hunting party from Amaldach-bre could testify to the solidness and power contained within those muscles.

Realizing that he was making a mockery of himself, Parrish stopped the posing and quickly made his way to the water side, people parting before him then gathering eagerly at his back, no one wanting to miss the smallest thing.

The man at the centre of everyone's attention eyed the flowing water with a practiced eye. In recent times he had completed more river crossings that he cared to remember. He doubted it would take more than a dozen good strokes to cross the deepest part and reach the high bank on the far side. Beyond it, the untrodden clearing that ended in forest looked green, fresh and clean. Almost as if waiting to be claimed. Something to aim at, he decided, a better reason to cross rather than purely for show.

The chill yet refreshing water splashed around his legs as he waded out into the flow, immediately soaking his buckskins and making them cling to him like a second skin. The riverbed shelved more steeply than he had first thought and in just a few steps he was in up to mid thigh. He turned, gave a loose salute to the watching crowd then, with a lunge of his arms, dived into the sparkling, clear coldness.

The icy sting of it on his skin made his eyes widen and he came to the surface with a great gasp, then laughed at the sheer delight of it. With no further thought to the awed spectators he struck forcibly out for the far bank, slicing through the water with a powerful crawl stroke, the kick of his legs churning the water white behind him. It was one more wonderful, life giving sensation to add to those he had just experienced with Juli. He had not felt so alive in a long time.

In much too short a time he reached the far bank and climbed up and onto the lush grass, water pouring off him, dripping from his hair and running off his buckskins that gripped him in their wet embrace. He turned to face his people, swept back his hair then opened his arms in a 'there you are' gesture before resting them on his hips, a picture of magnificence as he recovered his breath.

The faces of those on the far bank were full of amazement. Even Juli, who until he had started his swim had simply been filled with pride for her husband, was slack jawed in astonishment and at this impromptu display of appreciation Parrish felt a surge of self pride. He was about to shout across that he was on his way back now, with the intention of further impressing them with a spectacular dive back into the flow, when as one their faces changed from one of pleasure to one of sudden horror. Now they weren't looking at him, but behind him.

Naturally, he turned to look at what they could see, an act that saved his life. Still with his arms akimbo, the arrow that streaked towards the small of his back was blocked by his right forearm. In the process of turning, while he was in effect side on, the missile punched with a wet plop into his arm, high up near the elbow. He was saved a more lethal injury because, although the arrow did not hit the bone, the firm muscles of his arm stopped it passing right through and instead of striking him in the kidney area, it lodged tight in the limb. Even so, it struck with enough force to emerge from the inside of his arm by a good ten or twelve inches, the flint head and shaft glistening with blood, leaving the opposite, fletched end protruding away from the tight skin around the entry wound a somewhat shorter length.

There were cries of horror from some of the witnesses on the far bank while all Parrish could do was gasp as the pain hit him. Instinctively he clapped his hand to the wound, cradling his injured arm as tenderly as he could. Shoulders hunched against the sudden pain, he at last turned fully round and looked up to see where the cowardly shot had come from.

Standing on the far side of the clearing, having just emerged from the tree line, were three men. Even as he watched they slowly began to approach in line abreast. The two flanking men each carried bows, arrows ready nocked to the strings making it impossible to determine which of them had actually fired the shot. But it could only have been one of these two because the middle man carried no weapon, just a self satisfied grin. This one put out his arms to stay his two companions from firing any more arrows.

"No more." he spoke gruffly, greedily drinking in the sight of Parrish, his tall nemesis, cowering in pain and defeat. "He is wounded now, easy prey and will get no help from his people. I will kill him myself."

The pair obeyed the command instantly, dropping their bows but quickly drawing their battle axes, ready at a moment's notice to spring to the defence of their master.

Parrish just stared on in disbelief as the determined men approached, well aware that they meant him great harm but totally unaware of just who his assailants were.

But Klud knew.

"The Chieftain of Amaldach-bre!" he gasped and plunged urgently into the water in a valiant attempt to go to his stricken friend's aid. Several other warriors followed suit but all had to stop when the water swirled around their waists and they were then running the risk of putting themselves in peril too for no possible gain.

All the other members of the Danebury group stood transfixed at the horror they knew was about to unfold before them, unable to help in any way. All that was except for Tomps. With an almost superhuman effort he turned his back to his beloved Chieftain and ran off as fast as he could towards their makeshift camp. His weapons were there, for all the good they might do laying fifty meters back from the river, with another good forty meters further on across its expanse to go to where Parrish now stood all alone. Alone, injured and facing three warriors with death in their eyes.

The two Amaldach-bre warriors and their Chieftain closed with the tall man, still keeping almost shoulder to shoulder, the men only moving far enough apart to give their leader enough room to complete his intended task.

Turning his arm until the arrow sticking out of it pointed straight up, Parrish grasped the shaft from below, around the feather fletching. With a sharp twist of the wrist he snapped it off there, the splintered wood now flush with the skin. He gasped with the pain, more blood flowed from the injury and he hunched even lower into the position of defeat and dejection.

This pleased the Chieftain of Amaldach-bre all the more, eager now for the easy kill and the moment of sweet revenge. He stepped right up until he was but two paces from the now practically cowering Chieftain of Dane-bre, his two warriors backing him up on either side. This was too easy.

Back on the far bank the warriors and women could hardly bear to watch, aghast as their revered and until now unbeatable Chieftain cowered and submitted before his attackers. Klud too stood still in shock, thigh deep in the flowing but unheeded water. How could it be that his good friend and brave warrior was so easily defeated? Beaten, bowed and simply waiting for a shameful death.

It was fortunate then that he could not see the terrified rabbit stare that Parrish offered up to his main antagonist.

The crazed Chieftain glanced briefly away at the watching group and laughed out loud. He knew what they were thinking and it added to his enjoyment. Slowly, for full effect, he drew a flint dagger from the waistband of his tunic. His long awaited moment of revenge on the man who had destroyed his village and his seat of power was finally at hand.

At that same moment the look in Parrish's' eyes changed. He had succeeded and drawn them in close enough. Close enough to give himself at least half a chance. A fighting chance.

Simultaneously snapping up ramrod straight and taking one

massive step forward, he punched the Amaldach-bre Chieftain full in the face. Only able to use his left hand, the blow was not enough to knock the man out but he still went down, the dagger dropping from his grasp. Almost in one continuous movement the twentieth century man next swayed to his left, attacking the warrior there before he too could recover from his surprise. The smaller man never even managed to raise his axe in his own defence as Parrish took a hold of the arrow in his arm, grasping it close to the exit wound in an overhand grip. With an agonizing wrench he jerked it out of his flesh and, using the still exposed length of shaft with its flint head as a crude stiletto, punched it viciously into the side of the Neolithic man's neck. The force of the blow drove it completely through, severing the carotid arteries on both sides and slicing across the windpipe. The man died where he fell, gushing and gargling in bright red blood.

The people of Danebury were still transfixed on the river bank. Even their hardened Neolithic attitude to death had not prepared them for the sudden, explosive display of efficient and deadly violence they were now witnessing.

All that was except Tomps who had by now reached the camp, retrieved his bow, nocked an arrow to it and made ready to fire. From his more distant standpoint some ninety meters away he saw only three armed warriors about to kill his friend, mentor and Chieftain, who stood crouched and wounded before them. He was honour bound to do all he possibly could to at least lessen the odds in his friends favour. Although the small cluster of men were out at almost maximum range, he knew he must at least try.

In the very same moment that Parrish sprang into action, the young warrior released. His arrow arced its deadly way across the Gathering Point, over the heads of the watching crowd, over the river and on down into the little group beyond.

Only then realizing what was happening, Tomps was struck rigid with horror. In the time it took for the missile to complete its flight Parrish had downed two of his opponents and stood erect, looking for the third. Now Tomps' arrow seemed somehow to zero inexorably in on the tall man himself!

Unaware, Parrish spun from killing the warrior to the left, searching desperately for the second man. But this one had been afforded the luxury of a seconds recovery and now leapt into attack, axe raised in readiness.

Parrish knew he was beaten. It had been a good try but even his special combat skills, honed by constant training from the best hand-to-hand fighting experts of the British Army, could not protect him, wounded or not, against too great a number of fit, determined and armed opponents. The Amaldach-bre man stepped squarely in front of his twentieth century opponent, at once both drawing himself up to full height and closing for the kill.

There was a hard sounding thud and to Parrish's complete surprise the man never landed the intended blow but simply crumpled to the ground at his feet, twitching. Looking down at the fallen warrior he saw immediately the arrow that was lodged firmly in the man's back, high up between the shoulder blades. Amazed, he then looked up to see where the life saving shot had come from. Even those on the far bank spun to see, staring back at Temps.

The young warrior was still frozen in the act of release, that classic archers pose with bow held out and arrow hand at his chin. A look of complete horror was stretched taut across his ashen face. He knew only the action of the Amaldach-bre man, stepping in front of Parrish at the very last moment, had prevented him from putting his own arrow into the chest of his tall friend. How could he forgive himself? He was sure his Chieftain never would!

Parrish only had the briefest of moments to register the look on the boy's face. He was knocked violently to the ground from behind by the Chieftain of Amaldach-bre who, recovering from his assault and now insanely furious, leapt with an animal grunt onto the tall man's back and grappled with him on the ground, bare hands going straight for the throat.

Squirming around onto his back it was all Parrish could do to defend himself with his good arm against the smaller man who, because he did not gain an immediate success, began to scream and shout, cursing Parrish and threatening dire things against his person, wives, children and village.

Changing tactics to get the upper hand Parrish, instead of trying to push his attacker away as would normally be expected, pulled him close, rendering his blows ineffective. With a surprised gasp the Amaldach-bre Chieftain collapsed on top of him. Using superior weight and strength Parrish next executed a half roll and came up on top, sitting astride the Neolithic man who screamed in fury and began again to pummel him with his fists, the shouts now degenerating into mindless gibberish but increasing in volume.

Parrish gripped the madman about the throat with his weak hand and squeezed as hard as the pain would allow, while defending himself as best he could with his left. He knew he could not keep it up for long. The more he squeezed the more it hurt and the more blood flowed out of his arm. Plus the Chieftain of Amaldach-bre's blows were beginning to tell on his ribs and upper arms. And the noise! How the man screamed in blind fury, his voice now very high pitched and practically dripping with hatred and venom for the twentieth century man. As the man's blows assaulted Parrish's body, the insane screaming assaulted his mind.

Forming the fingers and thumb of his left hand into a tight cone, Parrish rammed his hand into the Neolithic man's open mouth, pushing down as hard as he could. The noise abruptly stopped and the man's eyes bulged in surprise. Parrish pushed with all his might, ignoring the teeth that now bit deeply into the back of his hand. The Chieftain of Amaldach-bre began gagging and beat his fists with ever more urgency against the body on top of him but the tall man could not be stopped. Still squeezing with his right as he pushed down with his left, Parrish was sure he could feel his fingers inside the man's throat against the palm of his right hand.

Then the smaller man vomited, the vile mess spraying over them both. And still Parrish pushed. The beating against his ribs increased briefly then slackened noticeably before the body beneath him began to jerk involuntarily. Both choking on his own vomit and suffocating through lack of air, the insane Chieftain of Amaldach-bre gave a massive shudder, jerked one more time, then died, his blood spattered arms at last dropping limp by his sides.

Parrish continued to push for a few seconds more before accepting the fact that the man was finally dead. Then he pulled his filth covered hand from out of the corpses face and rose slowly to his feet. He suddenly felt very tired.

The people on the far bank had watched the whole horrific event in total silence. They stared at their Chieftain as he stood alone among the bodies on the ground around him. Even Klud, who had seen many strange things done by his friend in the time he had lived among his people, found it hard to believe that he had just witnessed a man literally reach down another man's throat and pluck the life out of his body. Yet it had just happened, and there was no sound at all as his Chieftain stood there with his eyes closed, blood and vomit dripping from his battered body.

Parrish took several deep breaths, then turned his attention to the fallen warrior with the arrow in his back. He was totally motionless but gagging, definitely still alive. Kneeling beside the unfortunate man he briefly studied where the missile was embedded before looking directly into the man's eyes, whose face was turned toward him.

"I ... I cannot move." gasped the warrior, wide eyed terror and confusion on his face.

As Parrish had suspected, the arrow had lodged deep in the man's spine, severing the spinal cord and paralyzing him from the neck down.

"You are dead." was his cold reply. "I will help send you on your way to Dannu."

The last part was a lie because he knew that this man's skull would become a trophy and thus not enable him to sit in the great shrine hut of the Earth Goddess after his death. But he did not care. A few moments before, this same man had been intent on killing him and so he felt no pity. Besides, his injury placed him far beyond any human help.

Looking around he saw the dead Chieftains dagger and snatched it up. Without a word he pulled back the fallen man's head by the hair, once more ignoring the pain in his injured arm, and used the keen edged flint knife to deftly slit his throat. More blood spilled and then the last one was dead. It was a callous final act to the whole shocking drama but needed to be done and Parrish took some small crumb of satisfaction from the fact that because of the paralysis the man probably never felt it.

22

Leaving the three bodies where they lay, Parrish walked slowly back to the riverbank. He offered those opposite a weak smile, feeling no sense of victory although he knew his people would, then allowed himself to fall limply into the river with a great splash.

Some gasped at the thought that he might this time be carried away and drowned but after a few moments he came to the surface and struck out towards them.

Once again the coldness refreshed and revived his aching body and sinking spirit and by the time he emerged into the shallows of the Gathering Point he felt as if he had been washed clean. The only physical reminders of his fight were the tinted red streaks in the water being carried gently away by its flow and the fresh blood that flowed down his arm to drip from his finger ends. Klud helped him out onto dry land.

Now among his people once more they gathered close around him, waiting for him to speak. But Parrish uttered not a word. He looked past them all, simply watching as young Tomps, who had left the little cluster of wickiups as soon as he had seen his friend enter the river, approached the rear of the group then made his way slowly through. All parted before him and the youngster finally stood before his Chieftain. Although still horrified at what he had almost done, and humbled before his great leader, he stood straight and looked the tall man in the eye. He was a warrior too and would not shirk from what must surely come next.

"My Chieftain." he said softly. "I thought that I had killed you." He could say no more, speech failing him then. The thought of what had nearly happened jammed any other words painfully in his throat. There would be punishment now he knew, although just what he could not guess. Maybe even banishment from Dane-bre, but if that were his Chieftains wish he would carry out even that order with pride.

To his utter surprise Parrish broke into a smile and laid his good arm gently on the lad's shoulder.

"No, my young friend. It was your most impressive shot that saved me. Wounded as I was, I could not have beaten all of them at once." It was big headed of him to say such words but he knew the boy's deflated spirit needed urgent bolstering. "I am in your debt."

"Yes, it was a fine shot." agreed Klud.

"But it was nearly disaster!" cried the youngster. "If that man had not stepped in front of you at the last moment ..." his words tailed off, once again unable to speak the unspeakable.

"But he did." replied Parrish quickly. "Can you not see that Dannu guided your arrow? The man was not only my attacker, but my protector too."

The youngster just gave him a puzzled look and Parrish smiled again.

"Do not ponder on it my young friend, just accept that it is so and know this. As a reward, not only have you done a great service for your Chieftain, you have also gained yet one more trophy. For although I finished the man off, the victory is clearly yours."

"Hah!" shouted Klud and clapped the boy on the back. "Well done my young friend." All the other gathered warriors nodded vigorously in agreement.

Tomps gave a nervous grin, unsure whether or not to be fully deserving of the accolades.

Parrish was about to agree whole heartedly with his men's appreciation when someone took hold of his injured arm. Gentle as they were it still caused him to draw a sharp intake of breath against the sudden pain. He looked darkly down to see who caused this additional suffering and found Juli already beginning to apply a cloth bandage around his forearm to prevent any further loss of blood.

She looked up at him and their eyes met. No words needed to be spoken as Parrish suddenly realized just how terribly worried and frightened she must have been during the entire ordeal. Despite his punctured arm, bruised ribs and the deep bite marks in his hand he suddenly felt good, just to be with her again.

A warm, tender smile flowed onto his strong features and he softly touched the side of her pretty face. A brief return smile escaped from Juli before she masked it and continued to bandage his arm, as a dutiful wife should.

Brief, the exchange may have been, but all the people there saw and, as if it were a signal from Dannu herself, they all broke into cheerful grins, even the women of the group allowed this luxury without rebuke. There were several nods of agreement.

The old Parrish was back. How or why they didn't fully understand.

But neither did they care. It was simply enough to know that it was so.

Despite his injuries the Chieftain of Danebury decreed that everyone should be ready to leave the gathering Point as soon as the sun had reached its midday peak.

This set in motion a flurry of activity from all to be sure that they were ready when the signal was given to depart. Activity that included in particular a brief outing by the two warriors Klud and Tomps, who had the ‘honour’ of going the long way around to collect the most recently won trophies. It was by now well known that Parrish never collected his own, while his good friend and right hand man was more than glad to do so on his behalf. As the pair followed the line of the river back, three freshly severed heads swinging almost unnoticed at their sides, they had much to talk about concerning their strange and powerful Chieftain, a subject that was to continue unabated for some time among all the people, even when they were once again back behind the safety of Danebury's protective wall and ditch.

Another rich talking point was the fact that, as the village holy man had informed the high priests of Windmill Hill of the imminent departure, so had he returned with a personal message for Parrish. It had come direct from the lips of the wisest of the wise ones and the little Danebury shaman had repeated it out loud, exactly as it had been spoken to him. Every single person there hung breathlessly on each crisp, clear and proudly delivered word.

"It was well done, Parrish. Live long my friend and rule wisely. Till we meet once more. I say go with Dannu and farewell, my son."

The Neolithic people gave each other knowing nods. Proof once more, if proof were needed, that Dannu's man walked among them.

Parrish could picture the grey hair and those flashing eyes as the words had been spoken and felt a warm glow of satisfaction. He grinned widely, bowed to his holy man in respect of the words, then bade his people make ready to leave.

It was with the greatest satisfaction that Parrish finally lay back on his own bed in his own house in his own village and gazed thoughtfully up into his roof thatching. Juli noticed that this was something he regularly did after they had lain together and there was no doubt in her mind that there was some deep significance to it, although she knew her husband's clever thoughts were far beyond her. Seeming as if to read her mind, he at that moment patted her reassuringly on her bare hip.

It still pained him deeply to think of the loss of his unborn son but he sincerely hoped that might fade a little with the passing of time. Yet he knew too that things could have been worse, much worse.

On a much happier note, he was glad beyond words that he and Juli were once again an 'item'. It was clear to him also that there was great appreciation of this fact from the women of Danebury, which somehow made the day to day running of his village go that little bit smoother although none of his warriors seemed aware of this. They were much more interested in their victories and the celebration held in his honour inside the central shrine hut.

And what a celebration it was! Now their leader had a *second* mark of a Chieftain killer scored into his neck, a completely unheard of feat considering the very small number of villages and thus Chieftains on Dannu's land, and it quite rightly called for much feasting, dancing and storytelling. Not just this time from the old flint knapper either but particularly from Klud about his and Parrish's great chase across Dannu's wild south land's that ended in the defeat of the entire village of Amaldach-bre at the hands of the very warriors who now shared the hut with him. A great cheer punctured the air at this declaration.

Everyone was satisfied with the outcome of the chain of events that had begun with tragedy for their Chieftain, that final outcome in no small part due to the efforts of one particular tall man, they all knew. As far as the village was concerned things could not be better now the daily running of Dane-bre had at last returned to normal.

Gant had relinquished command of the village back to his safely returned Chieftain without a moment's remorse, regret or reluctance, something that Parrish was both touched and truly impressed by.

Tomps was the toast of the village because of his now legendary 'Chieftain saving' archery feat and the two additional trophies that hung in his stall. His personal tally of skulls now made him a much respected warrior among his peers.

When her chance arose Karin had flashed a discrete but heartfelt smile of gratitude across the crowded hut to Parrish, one that he accepted with a wink and the briefest of nods. A happy thank you for the continuing favour that her young, triumphant husband still gave her. In all honesty she did not envy her friend Juli living constantly so close to such a frightening, powerful man, but was none the less grateful that he was Chieftain of her village. A secret smile crossed her face then in realization that only now did she finally consider herself truly one of the clan of Dane-bre.

Klud of course was still good old boisterous Klud. Ruthless killer of his enemies, loyal friend of Parrish and personal advisor to the Chieftain of Dane- bre. As fast to appreciate another man's merits as he was to demonstrate his disapproval with his war club.

The little Danebury shaman presided over the whole celebration with a quiet authority that was appreciated and respected yet not oppressive, and all the time the Chieftain and his tiny wife watched the whole event with great pleasure and pride.

All in all things had not worked out too badly.

Parrish considered these things as he lay on his back before he finally propped himself up onto one elbow and gazed down on his naked wife. She smiled at him. With one finger he traced slow circles around her dark nipples and said quietly.

"I know that this might not be the right time but I thought you should know. As Chieftain it is still my duty to build my burial chamber to await the Earth Goddess after I am dead."

Juli went rigid, deep concern clouding her sweet features.

"Do not worry." He offered her a calming smile. "I just want to let you know that this time I intend to have the thing built as far to the north of the open plain as possible. Much closer to the great temple and with no chance of trouble from any other villages of the south lands."

The little Neolithic woman understood and smiled again. With an agreeing nod of the head to his wise words she snuggled closer, holding on with all her love to her tall husband.